TABITHA STRICKLAND

The Golden Wolf and the Stormwielder

First edition

ISBN: 979-8-218-66013-0

Proofreading by Miranda Hobbs
Editing by Miranda Hobbs

This book was professionally typeset on Reedsy.
Find out more at reedsy.com

Dear Mom,

Here is yet another book that you are absolutely NOT allowed to market at your church. Sorry, not sorry.

Contents

Preface

Some of the content in this work discusses—but does not graphically portray—topics that some may find triggering or distressing. These topics include but are not limited to:

Discussions around dubious consent and marital rape
Death of a parent
Reference to a still birth
Reference to maternal death in labor
Pressures to conceive

While the author does not consider the pregnancy plot point as a trigger, she is aware that others my find it distressing to come upon in the text. This is to disclose that a pregnancy between the main characters does occur at some point within the work.

Acknowledgments

Thank you to the online bookish community for always staying so thirsty. Spoiler alert: he plays with lightning, and she bites.

You're welcome.

Oh, one more thing…

Drink your water.

Introduction

Pronunciation Guide:

Below is a list of pronunciations for names found throughout the work. Some are names that can be found through website research, and others were created by me for this story. Pronunciations are listed in order of appearance in their respective categories.

Characters

Nilos: Nye-lohs
Anurob: Eh-nur-ob
Harvan: Har-vin
Shara: Shar-uh
Deidre: Dee-druh
Idris: Id-riss
Wreven: Rev-in
Karden: Kar-din
Brexten: Brecks-tin
Violet: Vye-oh-let
Azalea: Uh-zay-lee-uh
Jarrett: Jehr-it
Mikael: Mih-kale
Rallios: Ral-lee-ohs
Lowry: L-ow-ree
Alastrex: Uh-lass-treks

Crysa: Krih-suh
Silas: Sye-lis
Phillian: Fil-lee-in
Dawnia: Daw-n-yuh
Solaria: Soh-lar-ee-uh
Sylva: Sill-vuh
Robin: Rob-in
Juliette: Jool-ee-eht
Asha-anne: Ash-uh-an
Lyric: Leer-ik
Marcel: Mar-sell
Evalmir: Eh-vul-meer
Gretchlia: G-reh-tch-luh
Vadros: Vad-ros

Countries/Cities/Locations
Zelarum: Zuh-lar-um
Sardit: Sar-diht
Tyldon: Till-dun
Arcadius: Are-cade-ee-us
Heirlight: Air-lye-t
Vanar: Van-are
Crestmarch: Kreh-st-mar-k
Dawncliff: Daw-n-klif
Krislion: Kris-lee-on
Nirlas: Neer-lass

Dread Tidings

The morning air bit at his neck as Nilos lowered the hood of his heavy traveling cloak. The silver and sapphire banners atop the stables whipped against the sky, heralding the impending winter that would blanket his kingdom in white.

"Welcome home, Your Highness." One of the stable hands hurried forward, sliding the reins over Anurob's chestnut mane.

"It is good to be home." Nilos swung to the ground, his legs protesting after hours in the saddle. "Though, I return empty handed."

"We will find him," grunted Shara. The captain of his guard joined him on the ground and clapped him on the shoulder. "We only scouted the villages within a three-day range." Her hazel gaze shifted past him, her brow furrowing. "Perhaps the High General has word on Prince Harvan's next move."

Nilos turned, following her stare, and heaved a sigh at the sight lingering in the shadows of the palace. Even from a distance, the hourglass encircled with stars was unmistakable on the leather armor of the battle mages mingled with the royal guards.

"The High General never travels to Sardit unless it is urgent."

Nilos stripped off his riding gloves and handed them to a squire. "It took my own cousin murdering my father to draw him here a month ago."

Shara shook her head. "Whatever news he has must be too important or too hazardous to inform your mother via the scrying mirrors."

"We will find out soon enough," huffed Nilos. "Mother would have sent for me, once the gate guards alerted her to our return, if I was needed." He turned to his father's favorite steed and patted his neck. "Take the guard up to eat and rest. I want to see to Anurob's brushing and feeding my—"

"Your Highness!" Deidre's sharp voice rang across the courtyard.

Nilos whipped around to find his cousin and closest friend racing across the frosty grass. The morning sun blazed off her auburn hair, mirroring the fire magic that burned so fiercely in her veins.

"Deidre!" He sprinted towards her, prepared to catch her in a hug, but she slid to a stop. Nilos steadied her as she stumbled over her sage skirts. His mother's eldest niece was always excitable, but her brow was furrowed deeper than when Harvan's treason was made known to the Empire.

"Come quickly," panted Deidre, all pretense of a curtsy absent. Her fair cheeks flushed, and she gripped his hand. "Your mother needs you immediately."

"Has something happened?" asked Nilos, as Deidre tugged him towards the palace. He broke into a sprint to heed her urgency.

"The High General and his mages rode in this morning as if the very spirits of the Abyss were on their backs," she gasped. "They demanded the Empress be awoken at once, and they have been locked in the counsel room since." Her normally joyful eyes were tight.

"Have they located Harvan?" Nilos' legs objected to the strain of running after so long in the saddle, but he ignored the pain.

"I do not know!" Deidre shook her head.

The guards snapped to attention and yanked open the normally unguarded kitchen doors. Nilos dashed past them, startling the cooks, until his riding boots met the polished stone of the main foyer. He ducked a servant who hovered at eye level to dust a portrait frame.

Taking the main stairs two at a time, he reached the second floor and hooked a hard right. Deidre's gasped breaths were the only sign she was close behind.

The usual two guards outside the council chamber had been tripled with the High General's personal guard. Nilos paid them no mind when the palace guard heaved the iron reinforced, oaken doors open.

"This is where they were sighted," said High General Wreven tapping a map spread across the octagonal table. Ice crystals sparkled along the man's ebony hand and braids, melting as quickly as they formed when he rolled his shoulders to force his winter magic into control.

"Nilos." The relief in Idris' voice was palpable as she met his eyes. Her mahogany curls brushed her cheeks, framing the same hazel amber eyes as Deidre and his aunt Sylva. "You are alive! Thank the Star Makers."

The Empress of Zelarum pushed away from the table, and Nilos met her halfway into the room.

"Of course I am alive, Mother," gasped Nilos when she threw her arms around him and buried her face in his shoulder. The golden sparks of her solar magic hissed along his skin, drawing a rumble of thunder from the storm that slumbered in his own veins. He kissed her hair, ignoring the scrape of the crystal diadem. "I sent word to your guard at daybreak to let you know I was home. Did they not—"

"They did," sniffled the Empress. She pulled back, cupping his face and stroking her thumbs along his cheeks. "But something far worse than Harvan's betrayal has occurred, and I did not know how far into our land it has spread." Her eyes flared gold, as she shook her head. "If they had reached you, I do not know what I would have done."

"Mother." Nilos covered her hands and pulled them to his lips to kiss the signet ring there. "I am fine. I promise you." He kissed it again when she took a ragged breath and let it out in a trembling sigh.

"Your Majesty," said the High General. "Your Royal Highness. Please join me."

Nilos curled his arm around his mother and led her over to the commander of Zelarum's southern forces.

Ancient maps covered the war table. The crystals dotted across it glowed and pulsed along an all too familiar border.

Anger flared in his gut, coating his tongue in ozone.

"What has Tyldon done now?" growled Nilos, slamming his palms onto the table. Though Zelarum had never been directly attacked by their southern neighbor, the seven-hundred-year-old treaty between them had grown tenuous with each passing decade. "I shall slaughter the king with my bare hands if he has attacked us."

"It was not King Brexten," murmured Wreven. "A small village near the Heirlight mountains was attacked four days ago." His gloved fingers slid to a small dot on the map. "It was a small force, and they came during the night. They slaughtered nine families before a married pair of retired battle mages were able to repel them. They managed to kill one, but the others fled into the mountains."

He nodded to his mages, and one of them stepped forward with a black, leather sack in hand.

"This was taken from the one they managed to kill." The High General placed the sack in the center of the map and tugged the knotted string. It fell open, and the rage in Nilos' stomach turned to nausea at the sight and scent of its content.

Three eyes stared up from a bald head. Viscous goo coated the mottled skin, and short, tentacle like appendages framed its jaw and chin. The two eyes on either side of the nostril slits were milky white with pinpoints of black. The third took up the center of its forehead, as sickening blue as the lips of a frozen corpse. A stench more acrid than a skunkrat wafted up from it.

"What in the name of Star Makers is that?" coughed Nilos, resisting the urge to cover his nose and mouth.

"According to the historians of Arcadius," his mother hissed, "This is a Karden."

"A Karden?" Nilos laughed and crossed his arms. "They were annihilated centuries ago." Arching his eyebrow, he glanced between his mother and the High General. "The Karden are nothing more than scary stories for children now." He waved at the head, expecting them to agree to the impossibility they implied.

"They were not annihilated, Nilos." Idris shook her head and reached forward to cover the creature's face. "They were locked away in the wastelands of Vanar. The Rift was created to keep them there."

"Rubbish," scoffed Nilos, "Nothing can live in Vanar."

"Exactly the reason they were banished there." The High General passed the sack to one of his mages. "They should have perished without access to the outside world. The land there is barren. There are no lakes or rivers, no ground for farming. Even the sun cannot pierce the smog from the poisonous fire that spews from the earth." His fist balled on the table. "They should have gone extinct."

"Say this is a Karden." Nilos rubbed his own close-cropped hair in an effort to shake off the disbelief that pushed against the evidence being shoved in a larger sack. "If, against all probabilities, they did manage to survive a thousand years in an unlivable land, how did they make it through the Rift? It is sealed with ancient magic on our side of the barrier."

"I asked the very same question of the historians." The High General shook his head. "They had no answer, except that the page holding the details of the spell was stolen from the Lord Historian's library." Dread cloaked the space between them. "There is only one person from our land who would be bold or traitorous enough to take it."

"Harvan." The Empress breathed the name out, and the storm in Nilos' veins swirled to spark from his palms.

"We have to find him," snapped Nilos. His father's only nephew, the man Nilos had loved like a brother, had already proved he was capable of treason. "If he was willing to drive a dagger into the back of his own uncle and Emperor— my father, I do not doubt he would go as far us attempting to destroy the Rift."

"We must send a company and the best historians to the Rift," growled Idris. "We need to determine if he has, indeed, opened it or just used his twisted magic to deform some helpless citizens into whatever that monstrosity is."

"I sent a company to check." General Wreven straightened, brushing his shoulder-length braids back over his shoulder. "They should be reporting back by this evening. If this is happening, we need to warn King Brexten and Queen Violet. An alliance—"

"No." Nilos cut the general off. "We do not need them. If the Rift is open, we can handle this ourselves. Zelarum will not be dependent on the Mortclaw family for anything."

"Prince Nilos." Empress Idris's eyes glowed though her voice remained soft. "That is not your decision."

Nilos opened his mouth to object, but his mother held up her hand.

"You are not yet Emperor, so do not think to overstep your station." She lowered her hand, and Nilos snapped his jaw shut, swallowing against the tempest demanding release. "Son or not, you are still my subject. You will heed my edicts."

"As you command, my Empress." Nilos lowered his head in submission, though his every instinct warred against it.

"Leave us, Nilos," murmured his mother. "General Wreven and I must discuss things before we approach the council or Tyldon."

Nilos spun on his heel, shoving his way through the doors and startling the guard waiting outside.

The morning sun warmed Azalea's shoulders as she notched an arrow into her bow. Sinking closer to the dew-soaked boulder, she centered her weight. On her steady inhale, she drew her arm back, her prey unaware where it rooted along the undergrowth.

The wolf filling her soul crouched, lending her its sight and sharpening her hearing. She heeded its guidance. The wind shifted, blowing from behind her instead of towards her, and Azalea released.

With a sharp twang, the arrow's buzz filled her sensitive ears as it spiraled towards its target. She notched another arrow, letting it fly behind its partner just as the steel tip of the first embedded itself into the dawnhog's heart. The second pierced its eye, burrowing until the lilac fletching was barely visible.

It staggered forward, collapsing into the trunk of a tree, where its legs twitched twice before it let out its final groan. A scent teased her nostrils, betraying her own hunter before his voice rang out.

"Perfect shot, Princess!"

Princess Azalea lowered her bow and heaved a sigh as her stolen moment of isolation and success was interrupted.

"Must you follow me everywhere?" she shot back, shaking her head and leaping from the boulder.

Jarrett Tigersword's pristine smile and ochre eyes beamed down at her from his perch a few trees behind where she'd been. One leather clad leg dangled lazily as he waved the core of the sunfruit that he had apparently been enjoying while stalking her.

"Yes," he laughed and tossed the core over his shoulder. "It was part of the oath I swore on your thirteenth name day." He stretched along the thick limb, as lithe and graceful as the wildcat whose soul he had merged with. "Bloodsworn knight, remember, Your Highness." He rolled from the limb, falling fifteen feet to land in a crouch. "I swore to follow you to battle or the grave." He shrugged as he straightened, brushing his chestnut hair from his eyes. "And apparently, into the forest so you can foolishly hunt dawnhogs alone."

Turning on her heel, Azalea stomped to her kill and ripped the arrows from its body. The fletching of the one in the hog's eye dangled by splinters, adding to her irritation. She had spent all yesterday perfecting the flexibility and balance of her newest batch of arrows. Finding one so easily broken did not bode well for the other fifty.

"Oh, shut up," she growled, though the wolf in her core chuffed at the presence of its closest friend. She turned back to him, and her scowl could not remain as Jarrett emptied his pockets of half a dozen sunfruit and dropped them into the bag she'd left at the base of the boulder with a flourished bow.

"It is my job to keep Her Royal Highness safe." Her personal knight strode forward and nudged the dead hog with his boot. "What kind of knight would I be if I did not notice you climbing down a tower before dawn?"

"What if I was sneaking out to meet some secret lover?" she snorted, wiping the blood and brain matter from the steel tips on her shirt hem. "I do need privacy every now and again you know."

"Well, if you were coming out here to meet some mysterious man or woman," hummed Jarrett as he plucked the arrows from her grasp and dropped them into the quiver across her back. "It would be my duty—" he smirked at her, "to first test their endurance and skill in sensual combat in order to ensure they are fit to warm the bed of my Princess." Her knight winked and tapped the underside of her chin.

"You are impossibly crass." Azalea laughed and shoved him away.

"And yet, you have not ordered me executed," chuckled Jarrett. He bent, scooping the hog's legs around his shoulders. With a grunt, he staggered upright.

"I can carry that!" Azalea protested.

"You can carry the fruit." Jarrett snickered, bumping the bag with his boot. "It is not proper for a princess to haul a bloody pig into the castle grounds."

"To hell with propriety," grumbled Azalea under her breath. She slid her bow back over her shoulder until it slid into its slot in her quiver and shouldered her bag of morning supplies and sunfruit. "Since when have you cared about propriety between us outside of formal occasions, Captain Tigersword?"

"Good point." Jarrett flashed her another wink, and Azalea shook her head.

The companionable silence fell effortlessly between them, born of the eight years he had spent permanently affixed to her side, but it broke as they passed under the portcullis separating the cliff-side castle from the forest.

"Well that cannot be good," muttered Azalea. The scarlet and gold banners of General Beakpoint's personal escort shone from the shields of the warriors flanking the stables. "She never leaves Crestmarch unless father summons her, and he has not summoned her since the border skirmish with Zelarum five years ago."

"You read my mind Princess." Jarrett shook his head. "Let's take this to the kitchen and see what the maids know."

"The maids know all," mused Azalea.

They had barely stepped into the steamy room when Mikael,

her father's steward, plowed through the door on the opposite side of the kitchen.

"Princess Azalea." Mikael slammed his fist against his chest and bowed. "The King told me to inform you that you are needed in the war room immediately." Without another word, he turned and sprinted back into the castle proper.

Azalea blinked at the now empty doorway as Jarrett passed the boar off to one of the butcher boys.

"After you, Your Highness." Jarrett gestured towards the door.

"You have got blood on your cheek," said Azalea before dropping her quiver and bag in the corner of the kitchen and scurrying through the castle and across the entryway. The opaque, golden curtains billowed in the breeze carrying up from the sea below, but she paid no heed to the scent of the storm that tinged it.

Her soul-wolf prowled in her core, sniffing at the anger and fear that carried down the halls leading to the war room. If not for the scent of boar covering Jarrett's soul-tiger, she would not have known he was three paces behind.

The guards outside of the doors opened them wordlessly, and the Princess led her knight into the noisy room.

"Azalea! Jarrett!" Queen Violet exclaimed rushing over to flutter her hands anxiously over them. Her light brown curls were a mess, as if she had been twisting her waist length hair in her hands. "You are both all right. Where were you?"

"Hunting." Azalea gestured down at her leather pants, green tunic, and up to the thick, blonde, plait she'd tied around her brow. "We are having dawnhog for dinner."

"You are not to leave the castle grounds, with or without an escort, without telling us," snarled King Brexten. "You know better!"

Azalea touched Jarrett's shoulder to silence his low growl at the shout.

Her father's temper was never aimed at her, but his normally hazel eyes were as golden as the lion that prowled in his soul. Something was amiss.

"What happened, Papa?" asked Azalea as she slotted herself between her parents. She lowered her gaze to the maps, examining the outlines of their kingdom and of the Zelarum Empire to the north.

"What has that thrice blasted Rallios done now?" Jarrett's voice was low and threatening. "If you will let me, I will bring his head back on a spike."

"Emperor Rallios is dead," sighed the queen, gesturing to a small bit of paper unfolded on the map. "We received word this morning. Empress Idris now holds the throne, as decreed in Rallios' last will and testament."

"Then I shall bring you *her* head" Azalea fingered the dagger in her belt. "She cannot threaten our country." She was not grieved to hear the cold-hearted Emperor had joined his fathers in the Abyss. "I will bring her son's too, if you ask it of me."

"Zelarum is not the threat, Your Highness." General Lowry Beakpoint waved a hand. Her eagle sharp eyes flicked to Azalea. "We are facing something far worse." A soldier passed the general a scarlet bag tied with yellow twine. "Over the last week, two of our mountain villages have been attacked. One here—" she pointed to a dot on the map, "was laid to waste. Not a single person survived." She pointed to another. "This one here lost half the village before a passing party of soldiers rode into town seeking supplies and saved them."

General Beakpoint set the sack on the table and untied the strings

Azalea leaned forward, bracing her palms on the map as Jarrett mimicked her stance.

"Our soldiers said they had never seen such senseless slaughter." General Beakpoint shook her head. "The things that attacked, eight of them, were supernaturally strong. They ripped hearts straight out of chests as if they were nothing." She peeled the scarlet cloth away. "They managed to kill two before the rest fled back into the mountains. This is what we are fighting."

The final scrap of material fell away to reveal what Azalea could only deem an abomination.

Deep in her mind, the instincts of the wolf—her warrior animal, raised its hackles with a deep snarl.

"What in the name of the Sun Raisers is that?" she gasped. The deformed, three eyed, tentacled atrocity set her very skin on edge.

"The scholars say this is a Karden," said King Brexten.

"Ghost stories." Jarrett crossed his arms. "Shadow tales for fall nights. The Kardens died out centuries ago, when they were locked behind the Rift in the wastes of Vanar."

"Apparently not." Queen Violet's eyes narrowed as she rested her palm over Azalea's. "My tutor had a history book on the Abysmal War, and this exact painting was in the texts."

"We are awaiting contact from a squadron I sent to the Rift to scout the area." Commander Lowry busied herself with re-wrapping the head. "We will see what they report back."

"You know what this means?" King Brexten shook his head. The golden hair he'd passed to Azalea fell like a mane around his neck. "If the Rift is open, if they have returned, we need to reach out to Zelarum."

"I would rather be drawn and quartered," snapped Jarrett, "than seek the help of those egotistical, pretentious, spell casters."

"As would I." Azalea clenched her fists against the maps as she looked between her parents. Her battle-sight flared to life, tinging the room gold, at the thought of allying with the magicians to the north. "Give me command of a legion, Father. I will stop—"

"No!" Her father raised a hand. "You are heir, and, if there is war, you and your brother will be sent to Sun Temple Island."

"Alastrex is four!" shouted Azalea. "I am twenty-one summers! I belong on the war counsel! I am born for battle—"

"Captain Tigersword, remove her from the room," said her mother. "We must speak with Empress Idris, and Azalea's temper will not help us."

"I demand to be present!" Azalea howled when Jarrett's eyes glowed orange before he tossed her over her shoulder. "Put me down Jarrett!" She pounded her fists against his back, but her knight did not falter.

As soon as he lowered her in the hall, Azalea surged towards the door.

"Azi, no," grunted Jarrett, wrapping his arms around her chest, pinning her own to her side. "Do not even think about biting me."

With a snarl, Azalea latched her teeth into his forearm. Her knight roared in response, before he hauled her over his shoulder once more and carried her down the halls to her room.

Alliances Proposed

"Your Highness." A soft voice pierced the emptiness of Nilos' dreams. "Your Highness, wake up."

Nilos shot up from his heavy blankets, kicking them away. Goosebumps raised over his arms as his feet met the cold rug beside his bed. He pulled on a pair of fur lined loafers and tied his dressing robe around his waist.

"Come in, Crysa!" he called, snapping his fingers at the dark lamp beside his bed. Sparks met the charred wick, and it blazed to life.

The door creaked open, and a tanned face peeked around the gap. He waved her in, before scooping up an extra log and tossing it into the dying fire.

Lady Crysa Springheart, the healing mage apprenticing under his mother, stepped into the room. A sleeping wrap was still twisted around her head, and he yawned as she dipped into a soft curtsy.

"Is everything all right? You look like you were just dragged out of bed yourself." He rubbed his face, waiting for her to finish the sympathetic yawn she barely concealed behind her hand.

"Your mother wishes you to join her in her study." Crysa tightened her own robe around her. "The High General returned two hours ago, and she is with him now."

"Well, she would not have dragged you out of bed to bring me to her if it were good news," Nilos groaned. "Tell her I will be with her shortly." Crysa curtsied again before slipping out the door and closing it firmly.

He stripped off his dressing gown and pulled on the riding clothes he had laid out before turning in for the night. With an afterthought, Nilos plucked his platinum and sapphire coronet from its cushion on his desk and settled it over his head. For two days, the council had treated him like one of his adolescent prince cousins, instead of the twenty-seven-year-old heir to the throne, but if they wanted to drag him out of bed in the dark of night, he would remind them of his status.

Nilos did not bother with his lantern, navigating the darkened hallways by the familiar lure of his mother's solar magic. He paused, stiffening his shoulders, before opening the door of his mother's private office.

Empress Idris met his gaze from behind her desk. Her dark hair was loose beneath her own platinum and sapphire diadem, emphasizing the bags under her eyes. Whatever news the High General had brought must have been devastating, because he had only seen his mother's eyes so puffy and red-rimmed if she had been crying. The curtains over the balcony door billowed in the frigid wind, allowing him a glimpse of the High General at the rail.

"Mother," whispered Nilos, rushing across the room to kneel at her side. "What is wrong?" He brushed away the tear that escaped her right eye with his thumb. "Must I pluck the stars from the night sky and return them to your eyes?" Since he was a child, the question had always brought a smile to her lips, no matter how distressed she was. This time, its magic failed.

"The mages who went to the Rift," she croaked, taking his hand and resting her cheek in his rough palm, "They are all missing. Their horses returned to Arcadius covered in blood."

"By the Star Makers." Nilos' heart sank, and he kissed her brow.

General Wreven closed the doors behind him, and he placed the hand-held scrying mirror on the edge of the pale desk.

"We have just received word from a trading post on the border." He shook his head, coating them in a small flurry before he reigned his magic in. "Tyldon has been attacked as well. They lost a whole village and half of another."

"Have they requested a meeting?" Nilos stood, his hand moving up to his mother's shoulder.

"The rulers of Tyldon have not yet reached out to us since their last attack." The Empress sighed and stood.

"We are not initiating contact," snapped Nilos. "Mother, trust me on this. If we go to them for aid, they will turn the tables so that we will suffer the brunt of the loss. We must wait for them to reach out to us." He squeezed her shoulder. "Think of how fiercely they restricted access to their coasts last year."

"To which we cut the lumber and furs." She ran a hand through her hair. "I warned your father it was a foolish retaliation."

"I agree with the Prince." High General Wreven nodded, and Nilos inclined his chin in response. "We need to broker a truce that will be long lasting and result in equal effort in the days to come, and we cannot do that by initiating contact."

"I know that." The Empress smoothed her robe. "I just never thought that I would see this war renewed in my life, nor yours Nilos." She came around the desk to stare out the glass doors to the crisp sky above. "I just want what is best for my people."

The covered mirror on the wall above the roaring fireplace glistened beneath the opaque cloth and emitted a soft hum. The trio turned, their eyes drawn to the light.

The Empress waved two fingers, and golden dust spiraled from her hand. The tendrils wrapped around the cover, sliding it down to fold neatly in a nearby chair. The silver glass shimmered like a disturbed pool. Crysa's face came into focus.

"Your Majesty, Your Highness, High General." She dipped her chin in a nod. "The King and Queen of Tyldon are requesting an audience."

Nilos gritted his teeth and clenched his fist.

"Give me a moment." Idris grimaced looking down at her clothes.

"I have got it, Mother." Nilos dashed to the small closet where she kept a formal, fur cloak for unanticipated meetings and tugged it from its hook.

Gently, he wrapped the white and black snow panther pelt around her shoulders. Nilos stepped back as his mother fastened it with shaking fingers over her garments.

"Leave us, Nilos," she sighed, not meeting his eyes. "Please, just go. I will come find you when this is over."

"How do you expect me to negotiate with them in the future if you never—" Her weary eyes met his, and the silent plea stilled his tongue.

"As you wish, my Empress." Nilos bowed curtly at the waist before exiting the room only to collide with a pile of red hair and purple flannel.

"Whoops." Deidre righted them both as the door slammed shut.

"It is terribly impolite to listen at keyholes." Nilos draped an arm over her shoulder.

"Says the man who used to boost me up to look into the courtroom window every meeting day." She grinned. "What is going on? I only caught the last part," she whispered as they made their way back to his chambers. "What could King Brexten want? Are we going to war?"

"You are not going to believe it when I tell you." Nilos shook his head and waved her into the room. He kicked off his boots and threw himself onto the bed with a heavy sigh. Though his mother had sworn him and the advisors to secrecy until it was confirmed, there was no point in concealing it now.

"Try me," Deidre retorted, settling herself onto the large sofa under his window. "And take off that crown. You look like a fool."

"I could have you whipped for that." Nilos rolled his eyes, but he sat up and pulled it off. He twirled it between his fingers for a moment. "I may as well be blunt about it. The Kardens have returned, Dee."

"What are we, nine?" Deidre scoffed, helping herself to the decanter of Sunstill whiskey imported from the coast. "Tell me more. Have the mountain wisps begun snatching infants from their cradles?"

"Deidre! I am being serious." Nilos rolled over onto his side as he threw his pillow at his cousin. "We sent scouts to the Rift, but they disappeared. Their horses returned to Arcadius this evening covered in blood." As much as he loved her sardonic view of the world, the time for sarcasm was gone.

"Bloody star drops." Orange flames danced in her irises. "But the Rift? Is it sealed? It has to be sealed! Nobody would be mad enough to—" Nilos cut her off with a look. "Harvan bleeding Whitestar," she whispered. "He would never. Even he could not be as foolish as to risk the entire empire."

"We have no idea what he would do." Nilos sat up, crossing his legs, and rubbed his face. "Now my mother is brokering a treaty with Tyldon. They have been assaulted too."

"You should be there for that!" Deidre exclaimed, setting down her drink. "Why are you not in there? You are the Crown Prince for Star Makers' sake."

Nilos agreed with her, but he shrugged.

"You know why my mother dismissed me." He twirled his coronet between his hands again. "My distaste of the Tyldon nobility is no secret, though I maintain my courtesy when I broker agreements with their trade advisors." He dropped the coronet onto the sheets. "She thinks I will be rude."

"Well you are rude." Deidre gave a decidedly un-ladylike snort. "I could never decide who was more bullheaded, you or your father." She crossed her fingers over her heart and murmured. "May the stars keep him."

The pair lapsed into silence.

Nilos stared out the window, watching the clouds gather over Moonrise Peak. The celestial body for which it was named reflected off the snow-capped mountains, refracting its light onto the forest below. Frost gathered along the edges of the glass panes, bringing a mystical quality to the night beyond.

He glanced at Deidre, who stared at the fireplace making the dying embers dance and crackle with the absentminded twirl of her fingers.

A firm knock echoed from the door, and they both turned.

"It is open," Nilos called, stretching his legs out and letting them dangle over the bed. Deidre ceased her fire play and pulled her purple robe tighter around her.

The door swung open, and Empress Idris entered the room alone.

"Your Majesty." Deidre jumped to her feet and executed a low curtsy.

The wood door closed silently, and, as Nilos rose to bow, the sound reminded him too firmly of the tomb door that had sealed his father in six weeks past.

"Your Majesty." Nilos straightened himself when his mother's gentle hand cupped his stubbled jaw. Her eyes closed for a breath, and she swallowed visibly.

"Please sit," murmured Idris, patting the bed.

Nilos sank onto the blankets, the pain darkening her eyes chilling him more than the night could have.

"I will take my leave," murmured Deidre, edging towards the door.

"Stay." His mother settled beside him. "He is going to need a friend." She gestured to the blankets on Nilos' other side. "And please dispense with formalities, Deidre. You are family."

Deidre nodded and took her spot next to him, the warmth of her magic warring with the chill his mother's solemn expression had cast over his skin.

"What have you done, Mother?" asked Nilos, trying to hold her gaze.

"A truce guaranteed to secure a permanent alliance." Idris drew a breath and covered his hand. "We had to be certain that they would not abandon us. I need you to understand that the decision I made was to ensure that neither of our nations can ever abandon the other." His mother's eyes met his, tears filling them. "We need their armies, their trade routes, and their war experience. They need our magic, our lumber, and our knowledge." She swallowed again and squeezed his hand. "It was the only thing I could think of that would mean an unwavering alliance, and I do not expect you to be happy. I am sorry that this is how it must be, but there is no other way."

"Just tell us Aunt Idris," pleaded Deidre before Nilos could speak.

Not for the first time, Nilos was grateful for her bluntness and her friendship.

He returned his mother's gentle squeeze.

Nilos knew what was coming, before the words left her mouth. He could see it in her eyes as she glanced at his disheveled bed and his discarded crown. The ice settled into his stomach as his storm awoke with a hurricane gale in his veins. His anger was not at her, never at his mother, but at what his future was now doomed to hold.

"You are to marry Princess Azalea," said Idris. She wiped her cheek with her free hand. "We will meet them in Arcadius in one week for the hand-fasting." His mother cleared her throat. "Do you understand why?"

"Bringing the Princess into our lineage means that if the Tyldon abandons Zelarum then they abandon her." Nilos heaved a sigh. His soul and his magic raged against it, against having a choice he had not given thought to pursuing until the last six weeks, from his grasp.

"You hold no objections?" whispered Idris. "I expected you to have something to quip back or for your magic to turn the ceiling into a thunderstorm."

"For the protection of my people—" Nilos lifted her knuckles to his lips, pressing them against the sapphire signet ring on her right hand. "And for the safety of our family, I will do as my Empress commands."

"This is insane!" Azalea howled, spinning her sword in her hand as she squared off against Jarrett. "Me, married, can you even begin to imagine that?" She lunged forward, only to be blocked by his shield.

"I have a few times," grunted Jarrett. He pushed her sword away and struck her leg.

She blocked it with the flat of her own blade and pulled back.

"Well, mostly just of your wedding night." He circled around her, his smirk barely visible in his speed.

"Lecher," hissed Azalea. Spotting an opening on his left, she struck. Her strike rebounded off his padded armor with a thud. "I should have you flogged for saying that." She grinned as he flinched back for a moment, conceding the point before retaking his stance. "Two for me."

"But then who would you ogle at the lake." Jarrett laughed, bringing his blade to her leg.

She missed the block and huffed as her muscle absorbed what the pads did not.

"Your anger is distracting you," warned her knight. "It is clouding your wolf. You need to focus."

"I would like to see you focus after being woken up at three hours past midnight to be told you are being bartered off like a prized bitch in a property dispute!" Azalea snarled. She lashed out, her rage bitter and burning in her throat. "They took my choice! It was mine!" She had no more tears to waste, but her vision blurred, nonetheless.

Her arm throbbed when he slammed his elbow into her wrist, knocking her arm down. The dull edge of his sword stopped as soon as it met the side of her neck.

With a snarl, she surrendered to her wolf, refusing to give the tiger time to retake his place. Her blade met his ribs, propelling him backwards, and she pursued him.

Jarrett growled, catching her next strike on his shield and shoving her back. She surged forward with her own shield, the wooden discs shattering under the force of their mutual strength.

"Why are you taking it out on me?" snapped Jarrett, sweat beading across his brow. "I was right next to you objecting just as loudly."

"You are supposed to protect me!" She sobbed, striking out against him. "How can you protect me from a husband I did not choose!"

"I do not know!" roared Jarrett, slamming his blade into her thigh. The pain was negligible in her fury.

Tossing her sword aside as she staggered, Azalea surrendered fully to her wolf and lunged forward with the totality of her rage and fear.

Azalea slammed her elbow into his wrist, knocking his sword from his hands, and seized the front of his padded shirt. With a howl, she forced him back into the wooden panels of the arena walls. The orange glow of Jarrett's irises faded to their usual ochre, as she bared her teeth in his face.

His heart pounded against her fists, but her knight made no move to push her back.

"I hate you," she seethed, though she did not mean it. She could never mean it. His blood was too entwined with hers, bound by the Sun Raisers in Jarrett's oath, to ever truly hate him.

Her closest friend rolled his eyes and leaned forward to lick her cheek.

"Oh my gods!" Azalea yelped, glaring at him as she pulled away. "You are absolutely disgusting." She scraped her sleeve along her cheek as her battle rage dissipated into irritation. "I think I need to go soak in a salt bath now." Jarrett's mouth opened, but she raised her finger.

"Do not even say it," she warned and closed her eyes. With a deep breath she soothed the wolf back into sleep.

"I say nothing." Jarrett retrieved their swords. "But, in fear of being mauled again, I must remind you that your mother said she needed you to meet with the seamstress after training."

Azalea groaned as the fear and anger threatened to reawaken the wolf.

"I do not want to do this." Her complaints were useless, but he was the only one she could voice them to. The rest of the kingdom had to see her hold her chin high and sacrifice herself in the combat of marriage instead of a battlefield. "I absolutely loathe the snow."

They made their way to the armory and deposited their gear with the squires. Then together they washed the sweat from their skin with the lavender water waiting in a basin her ladies' maids filled.

"I know you hate the Whitestars," murmured Jarrett, tightening the strings on the back of the tunic she'd traded her training shirt for. "But this is for the best of Tyldon, Azalea. They cannot abandon us or harm you, or we cut off their trade routes and withdraw our soldiers." He spun her around and settled the delicate, golden, ivy diadem onto her head. Azalea clung to him as he pulled her into a hug. "I wish there was some way I could save you from this."

"You are coming with me, right?" she mumbled into his chest. He had no choice, she knew, but Azalea needed to hear it.

Jarrett pulled back and tugged an errant curl to get her to look up.

"Princess, I was fifteen when I bound myself by blood and honor to protect you." His voice was low as he smiled down at her. "After eight years of fulfilling that oath, do you honestly believe I would ever let you wander into the hands of Zelarum without me there to protect you?" His normally jovial eyes shone as they flashed between hers. "I would walk through the green fires of Vanar and back if it meant you would be safe." Jarrett kissed her forehead and rubbed her upper arms. "Now, enough with gloomy thoughts and doubts, let us go see what the queen and the seamstresses have planned."

Azalea nodded, trying not to sniffle at the blessing of a friend that the gods had seen fit to put in her life.

"What do you think he looks like?" She grasped onto the first thing to distract her mind from the doom hanging heavy over her heart.

"From what some of the advisors said, he's very handsome." Jarrett bumped her shoulder as they trudged into the castle. "Tall, a bit broody, very serious, and eyes like the winter sky." Azalea bumped his shoulder back "Sounds like my type of man. If you do not want to marry him, I could volunteer."

"Your type of man is anything with a pulse that consents," retorted Azalea. "You shall have no trouble keeping your bed warm during a blizzard." Over eight years, she had seen very few men or women immune to his charms. He had even brought her own mother to blushing during a dance or two.

Azalea had harbored a teenage crush when they first met, but the blood oath and her own maturity had doused that fire years before. Though she found the stories of his trysts amusing, she had no desire to bind her love to someone unsatisfied with monogamy.

"After you," whispered Jarrett before he opened the door to her suite.

Queen Violet's hands were planted on her hips surrounded by bolts of fabric and the castle seamstresses.

Azalea groaned inwardly at the sight of multiple corsets splayed out on her couch.

"I will wait outside." Jarrett murmured, giving her a shove through the door. "Good luck."

Azalea rolled her neck and straightened her posture as she made her way over to the women.

"Really Mama? You know I hate corsets."

"It is tradition," replied Violet pulling her into a hug. "Please, Azalea, do not make this anymore difficult than it already is." Her voice cracked, matching the trembling of her hands against Azalea's back.

"Please do not cry, Mama." Guilt washed through Azalea. She had been so caught up in her own misery she had not even considered the pain her parents must feel. "I know I have to do this."

She kissed her mother's cheek, and a few handmaids rushed forward and began peeling her clothes from her. Azalea did not object, trying to make sense of the chaos around her.

Heavy pants lined with seal fur were draped over her blankets. Skirts made of thick velvet and layers of flannel and cotton underneath were neatly stacked in travel trunks. Coats and cloaks designed to ward off the bitter cold of the winter she would be facing in a few short weeks hung from a rack that had been erected in front of her window seat.

Though she stood nearly nude, Azalea already suffocated under the layers that would replace the light, flowing wardrobe she wore for most of the year.

Queen Violet gasped, drawing attention to the dress being unwrapped from the waterproof oilskins it had been protected by for three years.

Her wedding dress was as pristine as it had been during her anointing ceremony on her eighteenth name day.

Per holy tradition, she had donned a white and golden dress and presented herself at the temple of the Sun. The priests and priestesses had prayed over her, anointing her with sea water and holy oil, asking the gods to bless her with wisdom, strength, and goodness. Then her father had crowned her his heir.

Azalea would never be queen of Tyldon, would never walk the aisle of the dawn to kneel under the rays of the Sun Raisers. The throne of Tyldon would pass to Alastrex.

Her throne awaited her somewhere in the north, in a palace she had never set foot in, in an Empire that loathed her. Azalea prayed that the gods understood why she must do this.

Swallowing her tears, Azalea shoved her pain away deep, burying it under her love for her people.

Somewhere in the lonely recesses of her soul, her wolf whined out the betrayal.

Vows That Bind

Nilos glowered at his reflection as he tugged at the black coat scratching his neck. It irked him to no end that he was not being permitted to join his own people in defense of their land.

While many of his fellow nobility led their bannermen to join the Tyldon forces or to the villages near Heirlight mountains to protect his country, his battle was to be waged in half an hour's time at an altar. Then he and his new bride would be forced back to Sardit to wait out the war while his mother joined the front lines.

As the only heir, unless his wedding night resulted in a child, royal decree forbade him from entering into combat. Instead he would rule the Empire in Idris's stead.

"You do what you must for your people," he reminded the scowling man in the mirror. "That's what Father always said."

Nilos pulled his wedding cloak from the hook beside the mirror, letting the blue snow panther fur run through his hands. He snapped it heavily onto his shoulders and fastened the silver chain around his neck. A knock echoed twice, and he welcomed the distraction from how much he resembled his father with the cloak on.

"Come in!" snapped Nilos.

The door opened, slowly exposing a wrinkled, wizened face he did not expect.

"Grandad Silas." Nilos blew out a breath, as his mother's father closed the door behind him.

The man produced a bottle from one pocket, and a heavy golden box balanced in his other hand.

"Oh my boy." Silas shook his head, shuffling forward. "You look so much like your father did when he married my little girl."

"Minus the adoring love-struck smile." There was no hiding the lack of joy in his chuckle. "So Mother chose you and not Uncle Philian?"

"Philian is leading my bannermen in my place," his grandfather replied. "If I cannot lead them into the defense of our empire, then it is my honor to anoint you for this journey." Age had not dimmed the wisdom or kindness in the old man's blue eyes, though it had turned his dark hair silver. "Come and kneel, my boy."

Nilos stopped an arm's length away and dropped to his knees.

"By all right, this should have been Rallios' honor," murmured his grandfather. "Or his father's, but they are with the Star Makers. So, I accept the right to prepare your soul and heart for the joining."

Silas placed the golden box on a nearby table and opened the bottle. The scent of moon lilies teased Nilos' senses, and he closed his eyes.

"May the Star Makers bless this man as he journeys into destiny." Silas dipped his finger in the oil and traced the circular patterns of their language onto his brow. The sultry aroma of the oil flooded his nose. "Bless his heart with fidelity." The circular pattern coated his brow again. "Bless his embrace with gentleness, comfort, and compassion." A third traced over the first two. "And bless their home with the laughter and love of children."

Nilos swallowed at the final blessing, forcing his fingers to remain open. In his distaste of the arrangements and the two subsequent attacks on both kingdoms, he had failed to even consider whether or not he would find his bride at least physically appealing enough to consummate their vows.

The cold, heavy weight of the traditional marriage crown passed down his father's line settled on his head. Even with his eyes closed, he could see it. In his youth, Nilos had memorized each platinum spike, each pure sapphire, and each initial carved along its band. After today, his initials would join his father's, and, should he ever have a son, so would his. Should he have no son, it would pass to his daughter's husband, and the line would continue.

His grandfather clapped him on his shoulders.

"Up you get, son," Silas whispered, his voice thick.

"Thank you, Granddad," replied Nilos as he stood.

He turned to the mirror and adjusted his cloak again. The sunlight caught the sapphires, casting fractals across the reflection before him.

"It feels wrong to wed at midday," he admitted. "It should be at moon rise, as the Star Makers stride the heavens."

"Imagine how your bride feels," replied Silas. "She should be walking down the aisle with the chariots of the Sun Raisers cresting the horizon to bathe her in the new dawn."

His bride.

The two words hammered against his mind, threatening to shatter the cage he'd locked his anger inside. Lighting flashed in his reflection's eyes, and the familiar taste of ozone coated his tongue.

"I need a drink," grunted Nilos, catching his grandfather's smirk in the mirror.

"Believe me, son, every man feels that way on his wedding day," Silas laughed before opening the door. "Now, your mother is waiting for you to greet Queen Violet."

Nilos rolled his shoulders and squeezed his grandfather's arm before he stepped into the hall of Arcadius's main temple. His guard fell into step behind him, something he'd become too accustomed to over the two weeks since the Kardens' first attack.

Empress Idris was impossible to miss at the entrance to the ceremonial hall. Her diadem coated the walls in sparkles where the sunlight refracted from the diamonds and sapphires.

The woman before her was a head shorter. An intricate crown of gold and rubies adorned the waves of her nearly brown hair. Even without the crown, Queen Violet would have been unmistakable with her sun-kissed skin and sword honed arms.

Clutching to the golden folds of the Tyldonian queen's gown was a boy of about four in black and scarlet, with a narrow golden circlet keeping his corn silk hair from his eyes. A jeweled scabbard that held a dagger no bigger than a letter opener dangled from his waist. He was young, but Nilos was more than aware he had begun training with the blade as soon as he was capable of walking. The boy's brows narrowed, and one hand fell from his mother's skirts to rest on the hilt of his dagger.

A smile finally tugged at Nilos' lips as he paused before the trio and showed his empty hands to the young Prince. His future brother-in-law released his dagger to once again cling to his mother's skirts.

"Mother," murmured Nilos, bowing low to his Empress to kiss her knuckles. He gave another bow, though nowhere near as deep, to Queen Violet. "Your Majesty."

"Violet, might I present my son, Nilos Asher Whitestar, the Stormwielder of Zelarum." Empress Idris gave a dazzling smile to the Queen. "Nilos, allow me to introduce Queen Violet Dawnia Mortclaw, the High Wolf of Tyldon."

"My pleasure to make your acquaintance," Nilos lied through a smile. "It is an honor to have you here on this day blessed by the gods of the North and of the South." Blessings would be if her daughter was slightly more fair than the mother.

Queen Violet was not ugly, but Nilos could find nothing in her appearance that would strike him as attractive either. If he was being forced to marry a woman against his heart and his will, he was sure the gods would not mind if he was shallow minded.

"King Brexten would have joined with us, but he is doing the ritual blessings and prayers over the Princess." Queen Violet's smile was as feigned as his own, but behind her pretense he caught the guarded sympathy directed towards his own mother. The Empress' eyes betrayed the same expression.

The monarchs had finally found a commonality, and it was the sacrifice of their children's hands in marriage for the safety of their people.

"I bet Captain Jarrett had to keep Azi from climbing out of the window again." Alastrex giggled from behind his mother's skirts.

Nilos raised an eyebrow.

"Is that something your sister does often?" he queried, fully aware he was breaking etiquette by addressing the Prince without his title.

"Only when she wants to go hunting without her guards." Alastrex's grin widened. "She's a really good huntress." The tiny Prince released his mother to hold his hands over his head. "You should have seen the dawnhog she brought home last week. It was almost as big as my chariot pony."

"Alastrex, enough." Queen Violet snapped her fingers at her son, but Nilos laughed at the glint in the boy's eyes.

So his wife would be a handful. He was eternally grateful for the unbridled tongues of children.

The sanctuary doors parted, and a priest bowed low.

"Your Majesties, Your Royal Highnesses, you may enter."

Falling back into character, Nilos extended his elbows to the ruling ladies and escorted them into the cathedral. At the altar, each woman released his arms and made their way to their appropriate seats. Assured they were settled, Nilos took his position at the base of the steps to the altar.

The silvers and blue of the Imperial banners were patterned between the scarlet and gold of Tyldon, the balance a juxtaposition of their seven-hundred years of distastes.

Slowly citizens of both countries filed into the room, taking up the wooden pews. Knights and battle mages lined the walls, holding position beneath the colors of the nations.

The doors closed, and Nilos swallowed. He flexed his hands, his heart pounding as the chatter of the room fell into silence.

The doors opened again, and a lone, armored man stepped into the doorway. The knight raised a trumpet to his lips, and the call that always heralded an emissary from Tyldon reverberated through the room.

Nilos nearly squinted from the gleam that radiated from the armor as he passed through the stained sun rays, until he caught sight of the emblem filigreed into his chest plate—a golden wolf with a crown of pink azaleas. A white cloak shimmered from a golden chain holding it to the man's shoulders. He held the knight's stare as the man approached, and the white, silk cloak stretched behind him, lining the stone floor of the aisle.

The knight's ochre stare was as frigid and lethal as the waters of the North Passage when he lowered the trumpet. There was no doubt that he was Princess Azalea's Bloodsworn warrior. He was sorely tempted to scan the room to locate Queen Violet's and King Brexten's warriors, but Nilos refused to break eye contact with the man who would spend nearly as much time with his bride as he would.

The knight raised his hand to his throat and unclasped the golden chain. He passed the cloth under his arm and knelt to place it on the stones. Then he stepped to the left, crossed an arm over his chest, and bowed to Nilos before turning to stride over to stand before a sword, shield, bow, and quiver resting at the edge of the altar.

As if a silent signal was given, everyone rose to their feet and turned to the open doors.

Nilos followed their attention, and he swallowed as King Brexten and Princess Azalea stepped into the archway. His heart sped into a marathon as his future began her slow march up the aisle.

The Princess's face was covered by a golden veil to show she had been checked for pregnancy prior to the ceremony, hiding her features from him. Golden beads radiated along her curves in rays of a new dawn, and Nilos' was oddly reminded of his mother's magic shining off of new snow. Her body, at least, was pleasing, with an ample bosom that led into a curved waist and spread out into strong, full hips.

The cloud of golden silk and white lace flowed around her like mist after the crashing of a wave at sunset. Her toned arms were bare, to symbolize both her honesty to her people and boast of the strength needed to lead her people to victory.

King Brexten's hazel eyes flashed gold as they drew close, and Nilos bowed at the waist to the monarch. The king lifted his daughter's right hand from his forearm and stretched it out to the Prince.

Nilos took it in his own, and Princess Azalea stepped forward and turned until she was profile to the congregation.

Drawing a breath to keep his heart from exploding from his chest, he lowered the Princess's hand and took the bottom of the golden veil in his fingers. Exhaling, he raised it, revealing his future, and eased it over her hair until it fluttered down her back.

The golden diadem above her honey blonde hair was nearly identical to her mother's, only adorned with pearls and diamonds instead of rubies.

Nilos lowered his gaze to her face, and his heart stuttered.

"You are a goddess," he breathed.

Nilos nearly smiled, until her amber eyes skewered him with such loathing that they froze his lips before they could move.

Azalea forced back the growl that swelled in her chest under Prince Nilos' wide-eyed stare. She had been unable to see him properly through her veil, but when their eyes locked, the wolf in her veins had objected to her body's response to the man before her.

People had said he was handsome, but he was as cold and perfect as the statue of Zelarum's Star Makers. His short, dark hair accentuated the winter sky blue of his irises. Both contrasted the warm strength of the fingers that guided her up the stairs to the waiting priest and priestess beside the altar.

His black uniform and the blue fur cloak were as imposing as the snow-capped mountains visible from the borderlands. The wolf in her soul raised its hackles, sniffing at the scent of a midnight storm that lingered just under his skin. He was enthralling—from his prominent ears to the proud, angular nose—and Azalea hated her stomach for the lilting swirl it gave when he turned once more to stare down at her.

That did not mean that she wanted him or to be his wife. This was duty, pure and simple, and she poured it into her eyes with all the fury she could summon. He was Zelarian. She was Tyldonian. Moonlight and ice could not exist with sunshine and sea. If he did not freeze her, she would melt him to vapor.

"Citizens of Zelarum," called the priestess.

"Citizens of Tyldon," echoed the priest.

"We are gathered today to witness the joining of hearts and the joining of nations," they said together.

Even though Azalea was not in danger, her soul-wolf prowled defensively in her thoughts. Battle raged in her veins, but she had no sword or bow. She had only her tongue, a tongue which was supposed to be repeating the prayer of blessing. Raising her voice, she declared the prayer she could not fully believe.

"I, Azalea Solaria Mortclaw—the Golden Wolf of Tyldon—do ask the Star Makers of the north and the Sun Raisers of the south to bless my heart and mind in accordance with their laws." Her voice carried out over the congregation below.

Azalea never took her eyes off the glacial pools above her. Lightning sparked within his pupils, as his lips fell into a thin line. She contemplated how much wine it would take to get him drunk enough to not consummate their marriage. Judging by his frame, more than would be socially acceptable at a wedding feast.

The northern burr of Nilos' Zelarian accent rolled over Azalea like thunderstorms on the coast as he repeated the prayer.

"I, Nilos Asher Whitestar—the Stormwielder of Zelarum—do ask the Star Makers of the north and the Sun Raisers of the south to bless my heart and mind in accordance with their laws."

Azalea raised her right hand in time with Nilos' left, as it would be from now until either of them died. The priest tied a gold and silver braid around their wrists, as the priestess anointed their foreheads with an intoxicating floral oil Azalea had never scented, but its sultry aroma stirred her soul-wolf into curious circles.

"Prince Nilos, your vows," said the priestess.

Azalea nearly protested, as Tyldonian vows were made in unison, but she silenced herself because she'd agreed to trade individual vows to secure their hand-fasting ribbons.

"I do, before all gods," declared Nilos, his eyes never straying from hers, "solemnly vow to protect the heart, mind, and body of my beloved." He squeezed the fingers of her bound hand. "I pledge myself as her protector, to ward her from those who would do her harm."

Nilos raised his unbound hand and caressed the air around her face. Bolts of lightning sparked from his fingers, and the smell of a summer storm washed over her face. A light mist swirled along her hair, settling against her neck and bare arms, and her heart skipped when she understood it was his magic. Her husband had warded her in the literal sense.

Azalea had never seen Zelarian magic in person before. It was as terrifying as it was breathtaking.

"I will honor and cherish her, seeking never to bring her to shame. I will love her and do all within my power to earn her love in return, so long as I reside in this realm." The miniature storm that gusted around her faded, and he lowered his hand to grasp her free one once more.

Azalea fought back the shiver his magic had drawn from her skin, but she could not stop her rebellious tongue from slipping across her lips to taste the flavor that dampened them. Nilos' lips twitched in the corner, his eyes softening for a breath.

"Princess Azalea, your vows," said the priest.

"I do, before all gods, solemnly vow to protect the heart, mind, and body of my beloved," swore Azalea, and her heart ached as she severed herself from her parents and homeland. "I pledge myself as the protector of his hearth, his heart, and any children I may bear to him."

At this oath, she heard Jarrett move behind her. From the corner of her eye, she counted first her bow, quiver, sword, and, finally, her shield being placed at the bottom of the altar, wrapped in the pelt of a golden wolf.

Nilos' brows furrowed, but she mimicked the same stroke of his face as he had given her. Azalea had no magic, but she was a battle wolf and would defend her pack with all that she had.

"I will honor and cherish him, seeking never to bring him shame," continued Azalea, lowering her fingers to his free palm as she squeezed their bound ones. "I will love him and do all within my power to earn his love in return, so long as I reside in this realm."

The priest and priestess stepped behind the altar and mixed two pitchers of wine into a goblet—grapes from her mother's vineyard and tart snowberries from his mother's garden.

As one, the priest and priestess raised the vessel above.

"May the Star Makers and the Sun Raisers bless this libation as they bless the marriage bed of these newly joined souls." They decreed, before the priest passed the goblet to Nilos.

"I offer you the seeds of my family," he murmured, pressing the goblet to Azalea's lips.

She sipped three times, savoring the tantalizing mixture of the wines before Nilos surrendered it to the priestess. Azalea accepted the goblet from the woman.

"I offer you the fertile soil of my family," whispered Azalea, pressing the goblet to his lips. Nilos' throat bobbed three times before she lowered and surrendered it to the priest.

"To sanctify this blessed union, and to symbolize your unfaltering devotion to each other," proclaimed the priestess.

"We ask the gods to witness the first display of your promise," finished the priest.

Azalea knew what was to happen next. It was the same in her traditions as his.

Her wine slaked tongue rebelled once more, slipping along her lips, and she arched her eyebrows when Nilos' gaze finally broke from hers to track the movement. Another bolt of lighting crackled silently in his pupils as they dilated.

She tilted her chin up when Nilos' fingers curled in a feather-light embrace around her bare arm. His eyes flicked between hers, as if waiting for her to prepare.

Azalea had no need to prepare. She'd spent the last week preparing, so she closed her eyes and leaned into his space.

Their lips met softly, and her breath caught at the gentle warmth. But Nilos pressed them firmly together and hauled her flush to his chest as his free arm curled around her waist. Azalea nipped his lower lip but found herself entirely unable to break away from the heat of his body.

Thunder echoed beyond the roof, and somewhere beyond the walls the howls of wolves joined the cacophony.

The gods, apparently, approved.

A Farewell of Grief

"Would you like more wine?" Nilos whispered to his silent bride.

The silver bread knife Azalea had been twirling between her fingers since dessert was served stilled, and she shook her head.

"Water?" Another soft shake, and the knife resumed its dance over and under her fingers. "Milk?" It was a foolish question, he knew, but it finally drew her honey-gold gaze back to his. "Are you ever going to speak to me?"

Azalea's left brow lifted, and his wife resumed her ceaseless scanning of the reception guests slowly emptying from the feasting hall.

Heaving a sigh, Nilos waved a server to the table and extended his goblet. It was nearly sunset, and the short feast was growing to a close. The urgency of their wedding and the rationed supplies had robbed him of the week-long celebration he should have been able to give his future Empress. Instead, he had been confined to a table with a bride as cold as the Crescent Bay Glacier.

Azalea bit the sides of her tongue as she soothed herself with the familiar motion of knife-twirling. If she let herself speak, she would break the alliance before it could be consummated.

She found Jarrett in the shadows, his palm on his hilt, and pushed back the urge to signal him to her side. His ochre eyes held hers, and he tilted his head before flicking his gaze towards her husband.

Husband.

The unearned—unproven—title beat a furious stain against her ribs in time to her racing heart, but objecting was out of the question. The sun was already below the high windows, and soon she would be locked away with him until sunrise.

Azalea's fingers faltered, and the blade clattered to her lap when the final guest was ushered away by the priest and priestess. She plucked it from her skirts and tossed it onto the white tablecloth beside the slice of cake she'd taken only one bite from. For the first time since she was a child, she wanted nothing more than to hurl herself in her father's arms and beg him to protect her.

As if her father had heard her silent plea, the Lion of Tyldon met her gaze and stood. Her mother joined him, and their apology pierced the space between the mages and knights stepping from their stations to partake in what was left of the food and drink.

A shimmer caught Nilos' attention from the corner of his eye, and his throat tightened at the tears filling the rim of his bride's feral, yellow gaze. The emotionless mask she had hidden behind through dinner was cracking, but the love and devotion that radiated from that simple change stirred something deep in his soul.

Prince Alastrex broke free of his mother's grasp and dashed across the feasting hall. Nilos yelped when the child kicked at a knight, dodged a mage, and leapt atop a table just before the elevated platform that held the wedding table.

"Rex!" Azalea surged from her chair, nearly catching Nilos in the jaw with her elbow, as she hurled herself around the table and caught her brother when he launched himself into the air with a despondent roar.

His Princess sank to her knees, cradling the lion cub in her arms.

Nilos shoved his chair back, raising his hands to stop the mages that swarmed towards the siblings.

"Please come with us, Azi," pleaded the Prince. "Please do not stay here. I love you. I do not want you to go."

Nilos rounded the table and waved his guard away without a word. His bride's charade had broken, and the tears coating her cheeks were, perhaps, the gentlest love he had witnessed in all his twenty-seven years.

"I have to, Alastrex." Azalea rocked her brother in her arms, and Nilos could not look away from her as she pulled the little boy's head from her shoulder and cupped his cheeks. "I know it is hard, but this is what it means to live for your people."

"Please, Azi." Alastrex buried his face into her neck again, the golden veil crinkling against her back in his tiny fists. "I will not let you. I will not let them take you away. I'll fight them all."

"Jarrett!" The howl that broke from Azalea's lips twisted Nilos' stomach. "Jarrett, take him!"

The knight, who had stared him down at the altar, strode forward and scooped the tiny Prince into his arms. Alastrex screamed, kicking and striking at the man's armor, while his sister wiped fiercely at her cheeks.

Nilos swallowed gasps when what he had considered a great sacrifice on his own part was shadowed by the truth of his bride's.

Azalea was leaving her family and friends, apart from her Bloodsworn warrior, behind. That had been her only request, the single thing she had asked his mother directly. Neither Idris nor Nilos dared to risk offending the Sun Raisers to break the divine bond.

Azalea bit the inside of her cheek when Queen Violet took the screaming Prince from Jarrett and handed him to his father. She keened silently as her mother whispered in Jarrett's ear before pressing a kiss to each of his temples. Both of her parents met her eyes for a breath before their knights surrounded them and escorted them from the hall.

She staggered to her feet, forcing her tears into submission and silencing the howling wolf in her core.

Warm fingers touched the small of her back, as the scent of ozone and fresh rain fell over her.

"Please do not touch me there," she hissed, jerking away from Prince Nilos' gentle touch. "You cannot begin to understand what I am feeling."

She regretted the words as soon as they left her lips. Her husband's hand disappeared, and grief tightened his icy stare.

Not two moons ago, Nilos had watched his father's body be sealed into a tomb. He knew loss, and he would never again hear his father's voice.

"I am sorry, Your Highness," whispered Azalea as she looked at her skirts. "Of course you understand losing someone you love."

"Please, Princess." Nilos' fingers curled around hers. "We are equals, both by birth, and now, by Zelarian law. You hold the same authority as I." He inclined his head. "Call me Nilos."

"I would rather not," huffed Azalea. Once again, she half-regretted it. Her husband was trying to be kind, but she was unsure of his sincerity.

"As my wife, it would be odd to have you address me so formally." His fingers tightened slightly as he closed the distance between them with a step.

"This is a formal occasion." Azalea turned her face from him and stepped away. Yet, she found herself unwilling to tug her hand from his feather-light grasp. It was the only thing keeping her from pulling the dagger from her cleavage and hurling it into the chest of the approaching Empress.

She curtsied low as Empress Idris stopped before them. Her new mother-in-law's willowy fingers brushed her cheek, as warm and graceful as a spring dawn.

"Welcome to Zelarum, Princess Azalea," murmured Idris, and Azalea resisted the urge to turn away from the woman's touch. "I cannot begin to comprehend the discomfort or grief you are concealing, but I assure you will be treated as if you were my daughter by blood and not by law."

"I appreciate your kindness, Your Majesty." Azalea had no ability to smile. It had fled in the wake of her family's departure.

Though both her nursemaid and her mother had told her of the Empress's compassion and kindness that balanced the late Emperor's stern demeanor, Azalea could not trust her so easily. Every fiber of her being was trained to suspect the Whitestars. Zelarians were as cold, deadly, and unpredictable as the winter storms that covered their capital each winter.

Azalea clenched her husband's hand, digging her nails in to keep herself from striking out.

As if sensing her discomfort, the Empress dropped her hand.

Nilos winced internally at the biting pain of his wife's grip. Had this been any other woman at his side, he would have brushed his thumb across hers or raised her knuckles to his lips to soothe her anxiety. But, it was not any other woman. It was Princess Azalea, and he would not let her believe she could battle him into submission to her anger. If she wished to silently war for dominance, he would remind her who she faced.

Nilos pressed his thumb into the meaty joint between her own thumb and forefinger, maintaining the pressure until her nails lifted from the valleys they dug into his skin.

"This is the Lady Deidre, my niece." His mother gestured to his cousin, where she stood a pace behind Jarrett. "For now, she will serve as your lady in waiting."

Nilos swallowed a snort when Deidre's brows shot to her hair, and her lips popped open in silent protest. His own bride seemed as nonplussed with the arrangement as his cousin.

"Until, of course, you find suitable handmaidens of your own choosing."

"Thank you, Your Majesty." Azalea's voice lacked all emotion. "Thank you, Lady Deidre."

Azalea's blank eyes shifted from Idris to the knight a few paces away, and Nilos was unsure what the simple narrowing of the man's brow meant. Either way, she blinked once, and the man's face resumed its blank mask.

"Perhaps Captain Tigersword and Lady Deidre are willing to escort the Princess and me to our chamber." Nilos was not looking forward to being locked in a room with her capricious temperament, but he sensed his wife may snap if she was forced to deal with anymore pleasantries. "Deidre can help her ready for bed, and the good knight can survey the security of the room."

"Of course, Nilos." His mother's smile returned. "I shall retire as well."

Azalea waited until Jarrett led them into the empty hall before she dropped Nilos' hand and reached in vain for her sword. Her palm met satin and lace instead of the hilt.

"I already had your immediate effects sent to your chambers." Jarrett assured her. "As well as your weapons."

"Thank you," she breathed and clenched her fist to keep from lacing her arm through his out of habit.

"This way," murmured Nilos, but Azalea did not reward him with her touch.

She held her head high, keeping step with him instead of trailing behind. She would savor the few minutes of freedom that were left before she would be forced to surrender to his hands.

With each step, the strings that bound her to her life snapped, and the chill that deepened the inner halls of the temple only irritated the wounds. When he paused before a heavy door and turned to Jarrett, she expected him to order her knight to stay in the hall. Instead, her husband opened it and stepped aside.

"If it will ease her mind and your distrust, Captain Tiger-sword, please inspect the chambers."

"I do not need your permission to ensure her safety," snapped Jarrett, but he stepped inside regardless.

Azalea counted her breaths until Jarrett returned and cupped her shoulder.

"It is secure and comfortable but chilly like the rest of the temple," he whispered. Jarrett's ochre eyes glowed orange. "There is plenty of wine, if you need it."

Azalea nodded, though she longed to beg him to throw her over his shoulder and drag her from the temple as her father had so often ordered him to do when she teetered on the edge of her control.

"Stay, until I…" the words caught in her throat. "Until Lady Deidre finishes helping me into my consummation gown."

"As you wish."

Azalea stepped past them into the room. The small hearth was not lit, and she wondered why, given the chill. Brushing it off, she passed the bed without looking at it. Once she was securely behind the dressing screen, she ripped her crown and veil from her hair and hurled them into the high back chair there.

"I know you do not want to do this but disrespecting your family's crown is unnecessary," hissed Deidre. Azalea spun to find the woman with her arms crossed. "My cousin is a good man." Azalea growled, and the woman prowled closer, fire dancing in her eyes. "Bloodying his hand was uncalled for." Her voice was so low Azalea doubted the men could hear.

"He's going to bloody my thighs before the night is through," she snarled. "It is only fair for him to feel a portion of what I will be subjected to for the rest of my life."

The fire in the woman's eyes vanished, and she drew a breath.

"Your point is well made, Your Highness." Deidre splayed her palms open as if in concession to the argument. "May I help you into your consummation gown?" Her hazel brown eyes drifted to the thin, translucent sheath that hung from a hook on the wall.

"Yes." Azalea warred against all of her instincts and turned her back to the woman. Deidre's fingers were gentle as she worked the buttons of the wedding dress loose, but the wolf in Azalea's soul growled warning regardless.

"I can place a protection spell on your wedding gown," offered Deidre. "Before I take it to be wrapped in the oilskins.

If I remember what I read, you are supposed to save it for your first daughter so she may choose what parts of it she wishes to add to her coming-of-age gown."

Azalea's distrust of the woman shrank by a sliver.

"Please." She stepped out of the gold and white pool of fabric at her feet and turned. Her husband's cousin lifted it from the stone floor and folded it with equally gentle care.

Deidre splayed her fingers in the air, centimeters above it, and flames danced along her skin. Azalea nearly shouted, but it died in her throat when the flames spilled onto the material and turned to a golden sheen that sank into the gown.

"It will be impervious to all but the most extreme flames," said the woman, a soft smile playing on her lips. "Now, turn for me, Your Highness. Allow me to help you into this."

Nilos shed his ceremonial cloak, unable to discern the whispers from behind the dark changing screen. With a snap of his fingers, it flew to the hook where it had hung earlier that morning.

The knight staring daggers into his chest scoffed.

"What?" asked Nilos, loosening his coat and tossing it onto a chair.

"Nothing, Your Highness," replied Jarrett, his voice thick and low.

"Liar," snorted Nilos, but he did not push the man. If Deidre were in Azalea's shoes, he would be as protective and irritable as Jarrett. The distaste between their people was too great for five hours of marriage to solve.

His wife's guard turned his head towards the changing screen, and he followed the man's glance.

Deidre stepped from around the screen, her arms ladened with the wedding gown, veil, and shoes Azalea had worn.

"Come with me, Captain," she hissed, shoving the knight towards the door. Nilos did not cower under the last, loathing glare Jarrett fired at him over his shoulder.

No sooner did the door slam shut and the lock click into place, than his neck hairs prickled. His magic swelled in warning. Nilos turned. His mouth ran dry by what he found waiting.

Azalea stood near the changing screen, her face as blank and pale as the first snow of the winter. The floor length gown did little to hide her ample breasts, supple hips, and powerful thighs. His blood pooled south before he could catch himself.

"You look…" Not once in his life had words fled him so completely.

Nilos had never been awkward around women. He had given and received pleasures of the hand and the mouth, but he had yet to take a woman fully to bed. The beauty that was his unexpected and unwanted wife, however, lit flutters in his core.

"I look what?" she hissed, her fingers flexing against the transparent material.

"Divine," he finished. "Azalea, you are a vision given form." Her whiskey brown eyes rolled, and he chuckled. "You are a goddess cloaked in mist on the first dawn of spring."

Azalea shivered, and his attention was drawn to the pebbled peaks at the swells of her breasts. He knew it was not arousal that had hardened them.

"Are you cold?" Nilos licked his lips to bring some moisture to his parched tongue.

"Yes." His bride finally wrapped her arms around herself, blocking the view of her breasts, and rubbed her biceps lightly.

Not daring to break away from her gaze, he extended his

hand towards the hearth. He snapped, measuring her reaction when the bolt of lightning shot from his fingers and licked flames along the wood inside. His bride did not flinch from the brief thunder that whispered when his magic faded.

Azalea stepped closer to the fire, and he moved aside to make room.

"Are you not going to change?" she asked, her gaze fixed on the burning logs.

"Right, of course." Nilos tore himself away from the tempting way the thin material cascaded over her rear. "I will be but a moment."

He hurried behind the screen, ripping off his uniform and cursing himself for so openly gawking at her. His new wife could not be comfortable with him displaying such an utter lack of control. Nilos took advantage of the brief moment to will his body into submission as he tied the strings of his pants.

Stepping around the screen, he found Azalea chugging from a goblet. The previously full decanter was nearly half empty.

"Well that is extremely lady like," laughed Nilos.

His wife's cheeks flushed as rich red as the liquid that dripped down her lips. He bit his knuckle to silence himself, while she snatched up a cloth and wiped her chin.

"Thirsty?" asked Azalea, a smile finally pulling at her sweet lips. She extended the goblet, and the edge of her lower lip caught between her teeth.

"Yes, actually." He took the goblet from her, pausing when his magic sparked wildly in his veins at the touch of her fingers against his own. The blush painting her cheeks darkened, and Azalea looked away. "Are you warmer now? I can add more wood to the fire if you need."

"I am." Azalea willed the wine to take effect as she stepped around him. The alcohol would stupor the wolf in her soul, and she would be able to leave her mind with what was about to come. She chanced a brush of his bare back with her fingers, and her heart leapt to her throat at the low hiss that slipped free from him.

Swallowing past the tightness, she folded the blankets back and stared at the white sheets beneath. The world turned, edging with stars, and her mind spun. Azalea did not know whether it was the wine or her own fear that caused it, and she ran her fingers across the sheets to steady herself.

"Are the sheets not to your liking?" asked Nilos. His voice was the same, soft, patient tone of a rider approaching a skittish horse. "They should be soft." He paused, but she could not look at him.

"No, they are fine," replied Azalea. They were as equally as soft as the ones on her bed back home, almost identical, and she wondered, but did not ask, if they were from a Tyldonian merchant. "Gorgeous really."

There was no more point in delaying the inevitable, and Azalea steeled herself. She had been educated on the intricacies of marital pleasure since she came of age, and Jarrett had never been cautious about recounting tales of his own adventures. So, drawing a breath, she climbed onto the high bed and knelt in the center, her gown pooling around her.

Nilos would have given every golden coin in the royal vault to know what thoughts twisted Azalea's previously emotion-less face into a rapid exchange of furious to timid to confused. He wondered if they were similar to the thoughts that filled him when her burning gaze met his—panic, uncertainty, need, and the sudden fear that he may not be able to perform to her satisfaction. He tossed back the last mouthful of wine and placed the goblet on the mantle.

He said nothing as he strode towards her, though her eyes roamed his body. Again, the corner of her lower lip caught in her teeth, and her blush returned with a quickening of her breaths.

He joined her, kneeling so their knees brushed and her hot breath broke over his chest.

"Do you at least find me physically appealing?" he asked. "I know we have no choice, either way, but I can always snuff the lamps and make it darker if you—" Her palm flew to his lips, and he sighed at the warm callouses.

"You are exceedingly attractive, Nilos," she replied. "That is not the issue, and you know this." Her voice was tight, dry and cracked. She lowered her hand and drew a deep breath. "Please, stop talking." He nodded, clenching his teeth together to make sense of the squinted way her honey eyes examined his face. "The wolf in my soul wants me to rip your throat out with my teeth, and, if I am to silence her enough to make it through this, I need you to let me familiarize her with your body."

Azalea's hand raised again, hovering over the hairs that spanned his chest. The warmth of her palm sent his already frantic pulse into a tumble. This close, he could not ignore the quickened race of her own visible in her neck.

Holding her stare, Nilos took her wrist in hand and silently pressed her palm over his heart.

Comfort of Compassion

Azalea had not felt like prey since she was old enough to swing a sword or fire a bow. The unfamiliar sensation did not sit well with her nor the wine hazed she-wolf that resided in her core.

Nilos' heart pounded as swiftly and ferociously as her own, and his quickened breaths rustled her hair. Thankfully, he remained silent as she slipped her hand along his body, memorizing the lean muscles and the static of magic that hummed just below the surface.

He did not touch her, and she was unsure why.

Did he not want to do this either? Had he lied about finding her beautiful? Did he prefer the company of men? Was that allowed in Zelarum the way it was in Tyldon? Perhaps, he simply did not find her shorter, more muscular stature as appealing as the tall, willowy women of his court.

"Do you not desire to touch me?" she murmured, avoiding his gaze to follow the path of dark hair down to the waist of his pants.

"Not until my wife asks it of me." Nilos' voice was low and graveled.

"That was not the question," she grumbled, but let his answer lie.

Azalea was uncertain she wanted the answer either way. Still, she continued the exploration of his body, until the wine had fully clouded her mind and silenced the protests of her wolf.

The defeat she was conceding hurt far less when her heart and mind were numbed by drink. Surrender came with little resistance when she could only focus on parts of her new husband's body—his pounding heart, his heated skin, his short, dark hair, the way his left ear was slightly higher than his right, the winter sky eyes that never broke away from her face, and the wine-soaked breath that spilled from his lips to whisper against her cheeks.

Azalea's muddled vision caught on that—the fuller lower lip—how his tongue slid along it. The memory of their gentle touch on her own at the altar drove her into movement. Whimpering, she surged forward and caught it between her own.

Nilos grunted at the unexpected lunge, but he caught his wife in his arms and met her kiss with equal fervor.

Azalea's soft sigh broke over his tongue as her lips parted, and he pulled her by her waist onto his lap. She curled her arms around him, her nails scraping against his back. Nilos clutched her closer, cupping her rear through her gown, as he broke from her lips to explore the satin expanse of her neck.

"Oh." His wife's breathy gasp and the immediate tilt of her head invited his blood to resume its previous course to his groin. Grinning into her skin, he laved his tongue over the flutter of her pulse.

"Tell me what you like," he murmured, nipping lightly at the juncture of her neck. "I want this to be as pleasurable for you as possible."

"What you are doing now," groaned Azalea, and Nilos rocked

up into her when she caught his ear in her teeth. "So, you do desire me, physically."

"There's something entirely too arousing about my wife being capable of snapping my neck with her bare hands if she so desired." The growl that accompanied her thighs tightening around his hips only served to harden his already yearning arousal. "Or her thighs, if she were feeling particularly merciful when I was dining upon her nectar."

"Would the mercy be the taste or the death?" Azalea's amber gaze burned into his when she tugged him away from her throat.

Nilos smirked, relieved to find she had found some amusement in their duty.

"Yes," he replied, and his wife's nails dug into his back.

"You infuriate me," she huffed. Her trembling palm cupped his neck, but before he could react she fell onto the pillows, pulling him by his throat over her.

"The feeling is mutual." Nilos stole her lips, and her fingers tightened for only a heartbeat before her hand fell to the strings of his trousers and untangled them. "Patience. Let me get you where you need to be."

"Do not tell me what to do," she snarled into his chin. "I am ready now."

"Damn it, Azalea," he grunted. One handed, he joined her in her efforts to push his trousers down, and he kicked them aside. "I may never have fully taken a woman to bed, but I know even fingers might be painful if she has not reached the peak of her arousal."

"I am prepared." Her thighs wrapped around his waist, and Nilos grunted when the head of his erection brushed against the heat of her thighs.

Azalea gritted her teeth, doing her best to recall everything her mother had coached her on throughout her life. She squeezed her eyes shut. There was a possibility of pain, yes. She was aware. She was supposed to give herself time, but the longer she touched him, the longer she drew out the inevitable moment, the more she wanted to scream and rage against the unfairness of it. She would not let Nilos Whitestar see her break.

"I shall be quick," her husband assured her, his lips gentle against her brow. She clutched the sheets, digging her nails into the soft, white fabric, and her mind filled with the image of them stained in her own blood. Then, she remembered Jarrett's advice about her wedding night and about finding mutual pleasure. Men preferred eye contact because they liked to see what their lover was feeling. It helped them understand if she may be concealing pain or discomfort.

Heaving a sigh, she opened her eyes and met Nilos' darkened gaze. His hand left her thigh, coming to frame her face on the opposite side to his other. His hard arousal stroked against her—lightly—in time to the labored breaths racking through his motionless body.

"No," he whispered. "No, I will not do this." He shook his head before dropping it onto the pillow beside her. "Azalea, I just watched every spark of defiance and battle drain from your eyes." He pressed the softest of kisses to her hair and rolled to the side. "I refuse to do this to you."

Azalea scrambled upright, her heart racing as her stomach sank to her toes. "We must, you fool."

"No," snapped Nilos, and her husband snatched up his trousers from the foot of the bed and tugged them on.

"By the gods." Azalea threw her hands in the air, glowering

at his bare back. "We are married. We must—"

"I was forced to be your husband!" shouted the Prince. He snatched the goblet from the mantle before turning to stare at her. "I will not let them force me to be your rapist."

His words crashed into her heart, twisting the dagger she had so vehemently refused to acknowledge. Lightning burst from his hair, singeing the short strands, and the metal goblet shattered in his fingers. She could not break away from his stare nor the maelstrom of emotions turning his skin and eyes to static of a summer storm.

"Damn it!" snarled Nilos, tossing the shattered goblet aside and jerking the decanter from the table. "Just go to bed, Azalea. I will join you when I am drunk enough to forgive myself for what I was about to do."

Azalea shoved through the panic that swirled in shadows around her vision, nearly stirring the unconscious wolf. She found her voice buried deep in the constricted narrow of her throat just as her husband sank into the high-backed chair near the hearth. She wanted to throw her arms around him and thank him for caring so deeply about her emotional state in so short a time. She wanted to stab him for so recklessly risking the welfare of her kingdom that their marriage had secured.

"You are a fool, Nilos." Azalea's dry laugh pierced the rage drumming in Nilos' ears. "A sweet fool, but a fool nonetheless."

"What are you talking about?" he scoffed before chugging from the lip of the decanter. The wine was nowhere near as succulent as her skin had tasted, but he would not treat himself to her again.

"They will check the sheets." The sound of her shuffling on the blankets drew his attention. "In the morning, Deidre and Jarrett will check the sheets and report back to the councils that we have consummated."

"Check the sheets for what?" Nilos finished the decanter and dropped it onto the table. Grumbling, he went to the cabinet near the mantle in search of more.

"My blood," snorted Azalea.

He whirled, finding his new bride crossed legged on the sheets, her arms folded over her chest. The flush from the wine across her cheeks emphasized the glassy urgency in her eyes.

"Blood?" He did not understand. None of his partners had ever bled from being pleasured by his tongue or fingers.

"Have you never deflowered a maiden before?" Her arms fell away, and her eyebrows lifted. "You said, earlier, that you had never taken a woman fully to bed, but you have been with a virgin in other ways, have you not?"

"No," admitted Nilos. "My past lovers were—" He tugged at his ear, and the burning static in his skin shifted to pool in his cheeks and up to singe the tip of his ears. "Well, they, ahem… they were…"

"Ladies of the taverns?" Azalea's lips twitched in the corner.

"No." He cleared his throat. "They were pleasure instructors." His own wife's eyes blew wide, and a bark of laughter made him jump. He waved his hands, his chest suddenly heavy. "Zelarian nobility hire pleasure instructors for their children when they come of age." Nilos did not expect her smirk to turn into a scowl. "It is to curb the foolish exploration that may result in illegitimate pregnancies or spread of disease."

"Oh, that is unbelievable." Azalea shook her head and pulled her knees to her chin. "I was robbed of my wedding week observing the pleasures of marital bliss between the priestess of Lyastra and their husbands, while you would have been off planning with your men how to kidnap me from the temple."

Nilos balked at the renewed bitterness in her tone.

"Kidnap you?" he asked, moving closer to the bed where his bride slammed her fist into the sheets.

"Yes, kidnap me!" She shook her head. "You would have had to best Jarrett in battle at the sanctuary door, then face me in combat, where I would inevitably yield once my desire of battle turned to desire for your body. Upon my surrender, you would steal me away until Father agreed to bless our marriage." Nilos eased himself to the edge of the mattress, stunned by the moisture pooling in her lower lashes. "How can I yield to you when you have not earned my surrender? You have not fought for me. You have not bled by my blade for the honor of my body, much less my heart. You have not proven yourself worthy to father my children."

The tears broke loose, flooding her cheeks, and Nilos clutched the sheets beneath his hand to keep from brushing them away.

"Azalea, I am sorry," he whispered.

"Now you will not even permit me to perform the one act that will ensure my family and people are safe from the Kardens." The slap came without warning, and Nilos hissed when it rang across his cheek. "You may not have been the one to rob me of my future, Nilos Stormwielder, but you are threatening the safety of everyone and everything I love."

Azalea snarled when her second slap was halted by Nilos' hand around her wrist.

"I *cannot* bed you, Azalea Golden Wolf, until you do it of your own volition." Nilos pinned her wrist to her legs, his eyes flashing. "I would never be rid of the guilt from the memory of you lying under me, absent from your mind and body, while I used you as nothing more than a repository for my lineage."

The passion in his heated whisper silenced her growled retort and quelled the urge to sink her teeth into his throat. Lightning crackled from his hair, meeting her skin in a static bite that tingled strangely pleasurable along her cheek.

"We must consummate," she whispered, tugging at her wrist. His fingers tightened, and another wave of static jolted up her arm. It pooled somewhere low in her core, kindling heat in her center. "If we try later, and are discovered, we court scandal."

"Then we shall title it noble, grant it lands, and host it in our halls," her husband growled. "I will not bed you this night."

"Then I shall send for Jarrett." Azalea yanked her arm away and scrambled from the bed. "I must be deflowered, and, if you will not perform, he is duty bound to do so in order to maintain my honor. He will never betray our secret."

Brief pain scorched along her scalp as she was yanked by her braid and hauled away from the door. The world spun around her, mingled with the vertigo of wine and the force of the tug, and she whimpered when her face was pressed into her husband's bare chest.

"I will not rape you," seethed Nilos, his fingers like vices on her waist as he lifted her and tossed her back onto the bed.

"It is not rape if I consent, you fool," she snapped.

"Consent under duress or out of duty is not consent, Azalea." Nilos' throat bobbed as he swallowed. "I will deflower you, but I will not rape you. You will not ask it of me. I will not torture myself with your pain. You will not take my soul's integrity."

Azalea started to question what he meant but silenced herself when he shoved her knees apart and pushed her dress to her hips.

"If you wish to stain these sheets to appease our parents, so be it."

"What are you doing?" she hissed, as the wolf stirred to growl drunkenly in her core.

"My hands will be bloody before this war is over," grumbled Nilos, and Azalea froze under the intensity of his stare where it focused on the exposed apex of her thighs. "I will stain them first tonight."

"I do not understand," she protested, pushing herself to her elbows.

"If sheathing my cock inside of you will make you bleed—" The fingers of his right hand slipped like silk along the inside of her thighs. "Then so, too, should my fingers."

Azalea bit her lip to subdue the snarl that filled her throat when he found the sensitive mound beneath the hair her handmaidens had trimmed and groomed for her wedding night.

"I shall be quick." Nilos dropped to his elbow over her as his fingers pressed at the entrance. "Bite down if it hurts. I accept the retaliation." He rocked forward, until his shoulder bumped her mouth.

"Nilos," protested Azalea, but he circled his fingers against her and kissed her left temple gently. The tender touches soothed her objections, and she closed her teeth over his shoulder.

"Ready?" he croaked into her ear. She bit harder, humming her ascent.

Discomfort washed through her as he jerked his hand forward. Azalea keened into his skin, grinding her teeth when her body tightened. There was pressure, and he growled into her hair, pulling his fingers back. She gasped at the relief, only to rip into his shoulder when he thrust his fingers again, and something tore low inside of her with a white-hot flash.

Nausea curled her stomach, and she clawed at his back. His fingers slipped in and out of her body in short, swift thrusts. She wanted to fight him away, to rid herself of the dry intrusion that burned her, but she could not. She had to lie still. Whining into the ozone and copper flavor flooding her tongue from her husband's body, she dug her heels into the blankets.

Then, the intrusion was gone. Azalea released her bite, falling back onto the pillows, and tears she did not want to shed scalded her cheeks.

Warm lips peppered her face, and sticky fingers tugged her gown back into place.

"I am sorry," repeated Nilos between each gentle kiss. "I am sorry. I know it hurts. I am sorry. Forgive me."

"I need a drink," she croaked, anything to have him away from her.

"You lie here," he said gently.

She hated that he had been right about her not being ready.

Nilos wiped his bloody fingers on the sheets, smearing as much as he could to mimic the movement of bodies during lovemaking. The sight of his wife's pain pooling into the thin material of her gown and spreading like a ruby puddle beneath her legs turned his lungs to ice.

He found a bottle of Frostpine gin tucked in a corner behind a bottle of Tyldonian wine. Grunting, he pulled both from the cabinet and popped the cork of the wine to fill her goblet. A bowl and rag for them to wash at dawn caught his eye, when he carried her drink to where she now sat, her knees once again tucked under her chin.

Once she was sipping it, eyes closed, he returned to the bowl and dipped the rag into the chilly water. Squeezing it free of the excess, he approached his blank eyed wife.

"Azi," he murmured. Her gaze met his, empty as it had been when they'd destroyed her masquerade of pleasure. "This should help with the pain." He extended the cool rag. "And so you do not have to feel anymore blood."

"Thank you," she replied, as flat as her expression, but her fingers did not extend to take it.

"Little wolf," he whispered, reaching out to stroke a lock of hair that had fallen from her braid. She blinked at him but did not respond. "Lie back. Allow me to tend the wound I dealt you."

Nilos was unsure his heart would ever defrost from the chill that seized it when she tossed her wine back and then sank to the sheets. She spread her legs, and he pressed the cloth between them as gently as he could manage. Then, so he did not startle her, he rolled the defeated warrior onto her side and pulled the blanket to her shoulder.

Silently, he doused the lamps as he chased his guilt away with the burn of the gin. Only then did he return to join her in the bed.

Azalea stared out at the pristine sky beyond her window. It looked no different from home, but the frigid air that sucked her joy was as foreign as the body behind her. The wind rattled the panes, but it did not make up for the absent crash of the ocean far below her bed. It could not soothe the incessant throb in her groin, though the cold cloth her husband had provided alleviated the heated swelling that had formed.

The wine sedated wolf chuffed irritably, longing to reach across the ocean at her back and sink its fangs into the storm that shared its nest. For the first time in her life, she smacked it, pushing it back into its den. She had no energy for its fury.

She was too cold and alone.

The stars rotated, slowly, until the huntress of the Star Makers peaked past the bottom edge of the window. The blankets and the fire did nothing to subdue the chill that swallowed her. Azalea could not quiet the shivers that seized control of her body.

"My Princess?" Nilos' voice was as hesitant as it was soft when it carried across the desolate emptiness behind her. "Are you cold?"

"Yes," she breathed with no desire to insult him over such an obvious question.

"I can hold you." Her husband's offer hung against her back like a fly buzzing along her brow. "Just hold you, nothing more. It is nearing midnight, and you have not slept."

Azalea rolled towards the heat of his skin, and she buried her face into his chest. His arms folded around her, cradling her head against his bicep, and his leg weighted her hip in place.

Enveloped in the furnace of his embrace, she sank silently into the grief of all she had lost, but she dared not let another tear soak his skin.

Song of the Wolf

The return trip to Sardit was not something Azalea was looking forward to. It was not that she did not enjoy being on the road or in the forests, but, apart from Jarrett, the only other people she knew in their twenty-person escort were Nilos and Deidre.

Her new lady in waiting had woken her early, sparing Azalea the discomfort of facing her husband after their wedding night debacle, and schooled her on the importance of dressing in layers to combat the frigid weather. When she'd joined her new husband in the courtyard of the temple, she had ignored the stares of his guard and their side-eyed whispers as she strapped her sword to her saddle and her bow and quiver to her back.

"You will not ride in the carriage?" asked Nilos, as she checked the stirrups on her mount. "This horse was to be an extra, in case Jarrett's came up lame."

"Are you riding in the carriage?" she quipped without looking at him.

"Of course not," replied her husband. "I ride with my mages, always."

"And now I ride with *our* mages," she hissed back. "Equal in authority, that is what you told me yesterday. If you are mounted, I am mounted." Without waiting for his protest, she swung herself into the saddle. Her husband stormed away, quite literally, leaving gusts of wind and whispers of clouds in his wake to take an older, dark haired woman with hazel eyes by the arm and whisper to her furiously.

"What was that—" began Jarrett, but Azalea cut him a sharp glance. "Very well."

She did not speak for the first length of their three-day journey, and Nilos seemed to have accepted her silence. His mages and Deidre followed his lead.

In their silence, she took to memorizing the route, the wildlife, and the shifting of the weather. By noon, she was thankful for Deidre's advice to dress in layers, though she did not speak it as she stripped off her heavier tunic on their brief pause to eat and water the horses.

At the first moon rise, a brief misting of rain mingled with ice crystals. She shivered silently near the fire, clutching warm wine Deidre handed her wordlessly. Azalea refused to retreat from the others until her husband or his guard captain, Shara, did the same.

She had begun to lose all feeling in the tip of her nose and her fingers when Nilos stood, extended his hand to her, and offered a soft smile.

"Come, my wolf," he murmured, drawing knowing looks from their escorts. "Allow me to warm you in the sanctuary of our tent."

Azalea tossed back her wine, before she took his hand and followed him into the darkened walls of their thick oil skin tent and the promising pile of furs laid out in the center.

She said nothing as she stripped out of her boots and weapons, before curling up on the edge of their fuzzy nest, wondering what their shadows must look like to those waiting by the fire.

Her husband shuttered the oil lantern hanging from a hook overhead before he curled himself around her tucking her head beneath his chin and pulled a blanket over them both in the darkness.

On the second day of their journey, Nilos was not ashamed nor loathed to admit he admired Azalea's tenacity. Despite her obvious discomfort in the ever-decreasing temperatures, his bride offered no complaint. That was, of course, if she spoke at all.

Every movement, every shift of her eyes, and every adjustment in her saddle came with a calculated, powerful grace. In the darkness of their tent, he had listened to her whimper and mewl in her dreams, sometimes calling for her mother, other times growling orders in a battle she had long since left behind. Her age and the vulnerability she kept locked away had been so palpable in their silence. Yet, it vanished the moment she tied on her sword belt and strapped her bow and quiver to her back.

Azalea would be—he had admitted to Deidre and Shara while his bride and her knight had slipped into the forest so she could relieve herself—an Empress like none their nation had ever known. They had looked at him like he was mad. He knew what they hoped, that the war that had caused the marriage would end swiftly, so the marriage could be declared unnecessary.

Observing Azalea without her knowledge was difficult, as her amber eyes never stilled. Neither, for that matter, did Jarrett's. It was not until the second nightfall that he was able to watch her without her keen battle-sight or the wolf that occasionally glowed a feral yellow in her eyes noticing.

Dinner scraps discarded, her sword was balanced on her knee. Jarrett nudged her, whispering something under his breath, and Azalea let out a shrill giggle.

His guards nearly fell off their logs, but she continued running the whetstone along the oiled planes of her blade.

"Do not be such a bore, Azalea, just sing," the knight chuckled.

Nilos froze, as she shook her head and looked down at her work. So his wife was musically inclined as well?

"I would like to hear it," he interjected, and the laughter in Jarrett's eyes vanished. "Had I known either of you were fond of song, I would have asked for a few flutes or crystal pipes to have been packed."

"Perhaps Jarrett should be the one to sing," she scoffed, examining her sword in the firelight.

"Anything to break the silence is welcome," muttered Deidre. "Except His Royal Highness. He could not find a tune with a tracking spell in broad daylight, much less carry it."

"And you called me rude." Nilos flicked a pea sized ball of lighting at her, grinning when it snapped against her sleeve.

"That was entirely uncalled for!" his cousin yelped, and Nilos ducked behind Shara as a tendril of the campfire snaked towards him.

From the corner of his eye, Azalea's scowl softened into a slow grin. There, in the corner of her lips, her tongue curled up to touch her teeth. It was, he thought, the most beautiful he had seen her.

"Fine, I shall sing, if you two will stop acting like school children." Azalea sheathed her sword, squeezing the belt straps in her palm.

The whispers of his guard stilled, as their new Princess took a sip from her water skin and drew a breath. Beside her, Jarrett rested his shield against the front of his knees and tapped out a steady rhythm.

Everything about Azalea seemed to melt as she closed her eyes and swayed her head in time to his drumming. Nilos was entranced at the change. Then, his bride tilted her head up to the waxing moon, and a mournful howl rolled from her lips and reverberated in the night. It brought to mind the wolves that denned and hunted near the northern passage, their white fur yellowing as winter retreated under spring's warm touch. She lowered her face, eyes still closed, and her words flowed like a spell.

"The dawn has come, so now I ride." Azalea's voice was deep, sultry in its smoky tone, holding none of the bird like notes he expected to hear. "Your heart calls me home unto your side."

Nilos leaned forward, drinking in the glow of peace that filled her face in the firelight.

"The battle won, all arrows fired," she continued, "To feel your kiss is all I—"

A separate howl pierced the night, silencing his wolf, and her eyes popped open.

Azalea leapt to her feet, her heart racing, and the wolf inside of her bounced in eager attention.

"Was that a wolf?" she gasped, spinning, trying to find the elusive creature in the trees. "Truly, a wolf? A live wolf?"

"Of course," laughed Nilos. Azalea turned to him, prickling at his amusement. "Wait, have you never seen nor heard a wolf, Azalea?"

"Wolves never come as far south as Dawncliff." She turned, still searching for the kin of the warrior that had bonded to her soul the moment she drew first breath. "The heat is too much, and when I visited the border, it was mid-summer so they—" the chuckles of his mages froze her in place. "Stop laughing at me!"

"Peace, my vicious warrior." Nilos stood, taking her hands. "First you sing for them, and now you show something other than outright disdain." His blue eyes flashed, as he raised her knuckles to his lips. Azalea almost jerked them away. The kindness in his touch was near to unbearable. "It is not mockery. It is surprise. Still your anger." His lips pressed into her knuckles again. "Would you like to see the wolf?"

"Yes," she breathed, searching his gaze for some sort of trick. "I would. You would take me to see it?"

"Grab your bow and quiver but leave your sword." He kissed her knuckles once more, and Azalea nearly tripped over herself as her soul-wolf yipped and bounced like a pup.

"I will carry it," said Jarrett, as he pulled her sword from the ground.

"No, stay," she instructed. "Your armor is too loud. It will be quicker with just he and I."

Nilos's mages and Captain Shara seemed to be of the same mind as Jarrett when they surged to their feet and convened on her husband.

"Neither of us shall be alone," said the Prince firmly. "Shara, Azalea is a capable warrior and, according to her brother, a skilled huntress. She is more than capable of protecting me, and I her." Azalea bit her lip to hold back the snort when he pushed past his guard to stare down Jarrett. "Captain Tigersword, I am armed with the force of a thunderstorm, and you know your Princess's prowess better than anyone here." Nilos inclined his head. "I will never allow her to come to harm."

"There may be Kardens," growled Jarrett. "Can either of you face them alone?"

"My mages have been running perimeter examination spells since we made camp, and they have detected nothing but a she-wolf just north of us."

Azalea did not wait for Jarrett to respond. She took Nilos by the hand, tugging him towards the forest in the direction of the howl.

It was not until the glow of the campfire had faded from view that her instincts flared in resistance to her foolish excitement. She was alone in the dark with a man she barely knew, one she had considered a near enemy since she was old enough to understand politics.

Her soul-wolf tensed, ceasing its ecstatic bounds, to sniff towards the storm crunching the icy leaves and grass beneath them. She jerked her hand away, nearly regretting her decision, but a scent caught on the breeze. Azalea's battle-sight flared to life, emphasizing the forest illuminated by the nearly full moon above the canopy.

She drew her bow, notching an arrow loosely, as she followed the trail of the wild predator and the human storm through the shadows.

Her husband's palms sparked and glowed, and a light mist twisted along his torso. She wondered how violent his storm could rage, or if he were only capable of emitting lightning and clouds. If she truly challenged him, would he turn it on her?

Nilos found himself quite unable to stop glancing at his own wolf as she stalked through the forest. That feral, yellow glow had returned to her normally amber eyes, and her steps grew silent despite her speed. The grace with which she moved, her bow drawn, was breathtaking. They reached the edge of a meadow, and she froze.

He stopped, biting back a smirk when she lifted her chin and sniffed the air. Wordlessly, she sank to her knee, and he crouched behind her.

"Do you smell something?" he whispered, and she gave a curt nod. "Animal?" She nodded again. "The wolf?" He took her replied huff as uncertainty. "Would you know a wolf's scent?" She huffed again. "Is it a scent you are familiar with?" Her braid rustled against his chest as she shook her head once. "Do you want me to cease speaking?" She nodded twice.

Nilos sank into silence, using the moment to observe how she lowered herself further and began to creep along the edge of the meadow without standing—a predator prowling.

He nearly stopped her, but the wind shifted, whirling around them until it blew from behind. Had she really smelled it turning before his storm magic sensed it? Nilos chastised himself when he realized he had been so caught up in her lethal beauty that he had ignored the tell-tale shift on the back of his neck.

They paused, again, and Azalea tensed before him when a shadow loped from the tree line across the meadow and stilled.

It made Azalea's spine crawl to feel Nilos behind her. Exposing her back to him on their wedding night had been in drunken anger. With full use of her mind, allowing him access to her vulnerability took every ounce of her control. Her distaste, however, was pushed aside by the silver and rust red fur rustling in the wind before her.

The wolf was larger than she expected, a head and shoulder higher than the guardian dogs that protected the royal livestock at their summer estate. Her yellow eyes drew Azalea in, lighting an unfamiliar yearning from the wolf in her soul. It wanted to run to her, to sniff her, to rub its head to her neck so their scents mingled and the bond of the pack blazed strong.

The she-wolf's angled face lifted, and she howled long and clear. Her song caught in Azalea's chest, sending her heart into a sprint, building in her own lungs until she could no longer resist. Releasing her bow to the forest floor, she tossed her head back to answer.

A hand slapped over her mouth, silencing her before she could utter a single note, and another wrapped around her wrist when she reached for the dagger in her boot to lay low her attacker.

"Have you lost all leave of your sense, Azalea?" growled Nilos, and her heart ached when the wolf sprinted back into the trees, startled by their scuffle.

Snarling, Azalea bit down on the bare hand muzzling her. Her husband yelped, and sparks exploded on her tongue, singeing it and sending stars across her vision. It jolted her heart into a strange rhythm. Blindly, she rocked her weight forward, heaving the man behind her over her shoulder, and yielded to the wolf who gave her life.

Pouncing on her prey, she pinned his wrists to the frigid dirt beside his head and closed her teeth over his throat.

Another, biting jolt lit up her mouth, accompanied by two more that shot through her arms and seized her muscles. They burst from her back, sending her skidding across the icy ground, and two furious balls of chaos shone down on her beneath scowling brows. Her wrists were ground into the leaves, and the weight and strength of thighs pinned her hips and legs in place.

The static pain faded, and the taste of a summer storm coated her tongue when it regained feeling. Nilos breath broke over her face where he panted above her, and Azalea's throat ran dry at the fury in his features.

"Come back to reason, Azalea," he snapped. "I am *not* your enemy."

"You used magic against me," she croaked, her heart racing as an unfamiliar warmth crept with a desperation to her lips.

"You tried to bite off my hand," panted Nilos, "and rip out my throat."

Azalea struggled against his grip on her wrists, her fingers hungry to feel his flesh beneath them. Nilos pushed them harder into the ground.

"I am not letting you up until I am certain you will not try to kill me." The warning clap of thunder that filled his voice lit a blazing hunger inside the wolf that Azalea had no word for.

She followed it, lifting her head to catch the lips of the tempest in her own. A pop of static burned along her chin, and she groaned at the pleasure it left in its wake.

"Again," she demanded and pulled at his lip with her teeth.

"What do you mean?" Nilos nearly released his wife at the sudden change in resistance, but he kept her pinned. The wolf still glowed behind her lashes, nipping at his jaw with a starving growl.

"Your lightning," gasped his wife into the underside of his chin. "I like how it feels when it sparks on my skin." He groaned into her lips as she kissed him, and Nilos obliged her with a short, teasing jolt. The throaty mewl she keened into his tongue and the way she shivered under him sent his blood flooding low. He released her wrists, losing himself in her frantic kiss when Azalea wrapped her arms around his back and fisted his cloak.

Nilos sent another, testing jolt of lightning as she nipped his lips once more, and, when his wife gasped, he dipped his tongue to meet hers, earning himself a deep, heady groan. She writhed under him, her touch wild against his shoulders.

He grunted, but did not release her, when she arched up and rolled him onto his back. His wild, ravenous wolf straddled him, grinding her hips as she chased more of the teasing shocks with nips and whimpers.

Nilos cupped her rear in one hand, guiding her lower down his body until she rutted against his arousal straining against his trousers. Had his subduing of her brought this on or was it simply battle lust responding to the pain of his magic? He did not know, but it felt too perfect to stop. How would Azalea react if he teased his magic elsewhere? Smirking into her breathy hum, he let a bolt loose as he squeezed the supple muscle of her rear.

Azalea hissed at the pain, pausing in her frantic chase of heated pleasure in her core. Her rear and lower back buzzed white hot, before sinking into the pins and needles of temporary numbness. Her heart mis-beat once more, making breathing difficult, and she broke from her blind feast of her husband's taste as the pleasure stopped short of tumbling over the peak of a precipice far higher than any she had reached on her own.

What was she doing rutting herself against the man who would not face her head on in combat? Why was she yielding so wantonly to a man who only showed his skills when her back was to him?

"Did I hurt you?" Nilos' pleasure-darkened eyes furrowed and softened all at once, confusing the wolf's lustful dance with its storm. "I did not mean to release that much magic. I was not thinking clearly."

"I should not have done this," she chastised herself, scrambling off of him and staggering to her bow. "I am sorry. I should not have kissed you."

"Never apologize for kissing me, you impossible woman," scoffed Nilos, and she could not look at him from her own shame burning in her chest when she walked past him.

"Azalea." His hand closed around her elbow, but she yanked her arm free. "Azalea, tell me what I did wrong."

She had no reply because it was not his wrongdoing. It was her own foolish response.

Nilos trailed after his wife, his mind reeling as he tried to decipher the inconsistency of her moods. In the pale moonlight, her furrowed expression and the slump of her shoulders were so unlike the confidence she with which she had previously carried herself. If he had thought her capable of it, he would have called it shame.

The smoke of the campfire had drifted towards them when the shadows shifted. The storm surged into his palms, and he barely kept it from releasing when a familiar pair of orange eyes came into focus.

"Easy, Your Highness," chuckled Jarrett as he held his hands up. "I mean no harm."

"What were you thinking, Captain?" snapped Nilos, as Azalea cupped her knight's face in both hands and gave a timid whimper. "I could have struck you down."

"What is wrong, my Lady?" The man ignored him, his gloved hands running along Azalea's messy hair. "Are you hurt? Are you injured? Did he dishonor you?" The glare that pierced Nilos' soul lit a roll of thunder in his chest.

"She attacked *me*," retorted Nilos, and Azalea clenched her fists when Jarrett stepped around her to face down the Prince. "I defended myself, but I did not harm her."

"The shame in her face says otherwise," snarled her tiger, and her husband met his anger with sparks in his hair and a maelstrom in his gaze. "Besmirching her honor is worse than bruising her skin, Stormwielder, and I will have the payment in your blood."

"Enough!" howled Azalea, ripping her knight back by his armor. "I will not have my husband and my knight measuring their cocks over my own foolish mistake."

"Azalea," both men protested, but she ignored them. Curling her arms around her stomach, she strode through their camp.

She did not like the conflicting emotions turning her wolf after its tail. Her body wanted something that her honor did not feel was earned, and Azalea did not desire to work it out in front of the company of mages sparking their magic as they prepared to rush to their Prince's defense.

"I am going to retire for the evening," she announced, tossing her braid as she lifted her chin. "Husband, you may join me or not. It is entirely up to you."

Nilos stared after his retreating bride. She disappeared into their tent, her shadow barely visible in the light of the single oil lamp within.

Deidre snorted, and he found her standing at the entrance to the tent she shared with Captain Shara.

"If you value your cockles, Your Highness," she laughed, "I would advise you join your wife as swiftly as possible."

"Noted," he grumbled and followed after the blonde conundrum that would be confounding him for the rest of his days.

Testing the Mettle

Azalea lay silently, her mind still a mess as she attempted to decipher the whirlwind of sensations and emotions she had experienced in the forest. Nilos had long since joined her in their tent, but she had not had words to give voice to the conflict waging in her heart.

Again, she was curled into his chest to hide from the chill. His heart thumped steadily against her brow, his breathing even, and his hands and leg were dead weight over her under the furs. The camp was silent, barring the occasional stomp of the horses or one of the guard mages adding a log to the fire.

She wanted to hate him. She had been raised to hate him, to despise him. His people had treated hers with disdain and intolerance because they found their love of battle appalling. Azalea knew he had been raised the same, under the false impression that her people did not love the written word or academic excellence as passionately as Zelarians. Yet, everything he did, unless she provoked him, was filled with compassion and concern. She had no bearing and no strategy to handle it. When he did respond to her antagonisms, the power he wielded was as controlled as his touches. Except, she noted, when she kissed him.

Any passionate response seemed to undo his control, and she

could not find the sense behind it. Yes, the physical evidence of his arousal had been present both times, but even then there had been so much consideration in his yearning touches. It infuriated her, and it sent her insides twisting in ways she was not certain she disliked. She needed answers because her observations of him had given her no tactics to respond.

"Nilos," she whispered, shifting higher on his arm. Her husband did not stir. "Nilos." Azalea raised her voice slightly. "Your Highness." Still, he remained quiet. Grunting under her breath, she twisted her head and bit down on his shoulder.

"Ow!" He yelped, jerking against her. "Did you just bite me?" Sleep slurred his voice, as he shifted away from her lips.

"Yes." She smirked in the dark when his hand moved from her back to rub the mark she knew she'd left.

"I was sleeping." He attempted to roll, but she tossed her leg over his hip and rested her head against his shoulder, pinning him in place on his back. "Did you bite me awake simply to achieve a more comfortable position?"

"No, I wanted to ask you a question." She felt his head lift from the rough pillow they shared.

"You did not have to bite me," grumbled Nilos, and Azalea chuckled when his hand returned to her back. "You could have said my name or nudged me."

"I did try, but you sleep like the dead," she replied. "Why are you so kind to me?"

"What?" His head hit the pillow with a thud, and she shifted her cheek so her lips brushed his ear.

"Why are you so kind to me?" she asked, again. "You should dislike me. Your people talk down on us. Your emissaries have never offered me more than the basics of courtesy."

"Allow me to clarify this," he yawned. She fought back her

own reflexive one. "You bit me awake to inquire as to why I am kind to you?"

"Yes," she said, enjoying the irritation that trembled through him.

"At this moment, I am contemplating being very unkind to you and banishing you to the carriage to sleep," snorted her husband even as the arm beneath her curled her tighter into his side. His fingers stroked lazily against her back, and the silence drew out between them.

"Have you no answer?" Azalea was certain the question would have elicited an immediate response, but her husband was delaying his words.

"I am kind because I see no benefit in subjecting you to more discomfort than you must already feel." His breath tickled along her brow when he turned his head and rested his chin on her hair. "Neither of us wanted this marriage, but I did not have to leave my home. I did not have to give up every aspect of my life, to sacrifice everyone and everything that brought me comfort and joy. You did. Why would I add to the pain and grief you already bear?"

Azalea swallowed, unsure how to respond to his explanation. She had thought, perhaps, his mother had ordered it or even some excuse that it was solely to maintain the alliance.

"Sweet wolf, I am kind to you because I vowed to you and the gods that I would do all within my power to protect your mind and your heart." His chin lifted from her hair, and she turned her focus to find his irises sparkling with his magic. "I vowed to honor and cherish you. That is why I am kind to you."

"You make it exceedingly difficult to hate you," she grumbled, giving her wolf lead to shine in her own eyes.

"Would you prefer I were rude?" chuckled Nilos. "I can be very rude. Deidre often tells me I am rudeness personified."

"Sometimes, yes," growled Azalea. "You confound me." She heaved a sigh, attempting to roll and turn her back to him, but Nilos hauled her back into place.

"I confound *you?*" Nilos scoffed at the narrowed, yellow glare below him. "Says the woman who first attempts to rip out my throat and then kisses me to the point of nearly losing control."

"I apologized for that," protested Azalea. If he did not have her confined in his arms, Nilos was certain she would have crossed her own.

"And I told you that no apology was necessary," he murmured. "In fact, I have no complaints. I encourage you to kiss me again, whenever and wherever you desire. We can avoid the part where you attempt to murder me."

"What if I never again desire to kiss you?" The question came with no emotion or hint of humor, and Nilos' stomach knotted.

"Then we shall never kiss again," he replied.

"Why does that make me desire to both kiss you and strangle you?" Azalea's question caught him off guard, so different from her previous, unpredictable interrogation.

"We have discussed that attempting to kill me is off limits," he chuckled, and his laughter died when her lips met his in a whispered brush. His magic flared, once again popping between their mouths at the unexpected contact.

"I should only want to strangle you," whimpered his wife, as she slid her hands up to stroke his cheek. "But—" Nilos cradled the back of her head when she silenced herself by brushing her tongue along his for a brief moment.

"But what, my gentle wolf?" he groaned, seizing her thigh and pulling it higher so he might turn and cradle her trembling body closer beneath the furs.

"When I feel your powers," she gasped, rocking against him. Nilos eagerly welcomed the return of her lips to his and allowed his magic to spark into her skin. "It robs me of all thought but our bodies together and of your touch on my skin."

He silenced her this time, rolling his hungry wolf onto her back and slotting himself between her thighs. Eagerly, he laced their fingers together on the pillow, easing his powers with gentle currents into her palms as she arched beneath him.

"You are the only lover who has found the bite of my lightning arousing," he groaned into her throat. Her powerful thighs curled around his hips, and he rocked forward, earning himself a graveled growl from his Princess. "I must always keep it in check, but you catch me unawares. And I find I cannot restrain it."

"I want to hate you," she whimpered, and Nilos hissed when her teeth scraped along his jaw. The sensation in their wake was strangely enticing, clearing his drowsy thoughts with simmering need. "Gods, I want to hate you."

"Then hate me," he permitted before tempting another shaky whimper by rocking his hips into her center. "Hate me with every fiber of your being, my Princess, but never cease kissing me so furiously."

His wife heeded his command with such force that their teeth clacked together. He graced her with a slightly stronger wave of power, groaning when her arms spasmed beneath his own, and her heels dug into his rear.

He broke from her lips, catching her ear between his teeth

and rolled his length against the heat spreading through the material hiding her sweet center from him.

"Bite me," ordered Nilos. Azalea met his movement with a grind of her hips, rocking herself against him, and keened wordlessly into his neck. "I said *bite me.*"

Pain flashed red pleasure across his eyelids when his wife latched onto his neck with a growl. Her fingers dug into his shirt, and her sharp nails dragged through the material. He knew she would leave welts, but if this is what it took to fuel her need, he would gladly give it. Nilos had no intention to consummate their marriage in the forest with only a wall of cloth shielding them from the others, but he would drive her to climax if he could. He wanted to feel her, see her wild beneath him, and hear her howl his name.

She was close. He could feel it, taste it in the heat of her skin and the frantic gasps into his tongue when he stole her passion in a kiss.

Without warning he was on his back, and Azalea had tossed the furs aside.

"What—" he yelped, but his protest was silenced by a shout from somewhere in the camp.

A flash of blue lit up the tent walls, and Azalea had her quiver across her back and bow in hand before he could blink.

"Kardens!" roared a voice, deep and commanding, and, as Nilos' thoughts cleared from lust to panic, he realized it was Jarrett's.

His warrior Princess had already darted from the tent, and Nilos ripped his own, rarely used, sword from its sheath. He barreled after her, wincing as another flash of blue blinded him.

Shouting, he gave into the storm and hurled a strike at the

mottled, tentacled face barreling towards him. The lighting crashed into its chest, sending it flying into a tree. Before he could blink, Captain Shara's back was pressed to his, and they circled together to face their foe.

Azalea longed for her sword, but there were too many enemies between her and Jarrett's tent. Her tiger was slashing away, Deidre at his side hurling fire like comets at their enemy. The combat was too close-quarters to effectively fire an arrow, so she sprinted to the heavy, armored carriage that contained their extra supplies instead of her.

She leaped onto one of the wheels then up to the roof, taking aim at one of the abominations as the eye of its forehead opened and began to glow sickeningly white-blue. With a snarl, she released an arrow, and the blue light exploded out, bursting the creature's skull like an overripe melon dropped from a wagon.

"The blue eye!" commanded Azalea. "Aim for the third eye!"

She unleashed arrow after arrow, some finding their target in the strange creature's power center. Others she sent flying to slow them from felling one of the mages.

A clap of thunder nearly toppled her from her perch when her storm embedded his blade into the chest of one of the creatures. Lighting surged through him, hiding him in purple-white flashes as the creature seized and flailed against the dirt.

A tent was on fire. Horses screamed, and Azalea's stomach twisted with a pain she had only felt once before. She found her stance, readying one of her remaining two arrows, in time to find her Bloodsworn knight in the glow of a Karden's blast.

Her arrow sank into the creature's neck. Deidre came in swiftly, slamming her flaming hands into its face as it clawed at the arrow, and its head exploded. The corpse crumpled into fiery rags.

Jarrett's sword pierced the eye of the one in front of him.

The wolf snapped its attention to the side, seeking her Prince, her unrelenting tempest.

He stood over a wounded mage, his sword feet away, both hands raised to the thunderheads swirling above him. The two remaining Kardens stalked towards him, claws dripping, lips pulled back in snarls. The one in front opened its eye, as its companion sneered behind it.

"You will *not* touch him!" howled Azalea and her wolf, and the last arrow ripped from her bow.

It spiraled through the air, passing by her husband's ear, and was swallowed by the lighting that he hurled with a deafening boom of his hands.

It pierced the eye of the first—as the lightning flowed down its body—erupted from its skull, and embedded itself in the eye of the other. The lightning flashed at the moment both creatures exploded, knocking her to her knees.

Thunder rumbled around them in time to her Prince's heaving shoulders. It faded, plunging them into silence thick with finality.

Azalea spat her fury to the ground below before she tossed back her head and howled her victory to the sky.

Below her, her Bloodsworn tiger roared, challenging all within hearing distance to test them again.

She let loose another howl, warning any creature or person in the forest that she rode her victory and would taste another given the chance.

Nilos spun after helping Robin, the guards' healing mage, to his feet. His spine crawled at the animalistic bellows, but the sight waiting for him erased the fear.

Captain Tigersword held Deidre up right with one arm, his

cousin's arm cradled to her chest. His other hand was raised, sword brandished high, dripping with the thick, gray blood of their enemy.

That was not what he sought, though, and his storm gusted wildly in his veins when he found his wolf.

Azalea knelt on the roof of the carriage, her head tossed back, singing her victory to the night. When it lulled, the night responded with howls of the wild wolves—heralding their sister—singing to her in words he could never hope to understand. He knew what the feeling they brought was, because the wind around the camp sang it to his soul.

Grinning, he crossed the camp to his pride, his Princess, his wolf, and she met him with a glowing, yellow grin.

Nilos caught her when she leapt from the roof, tossing her arms around his neck, and he barely felt her bow smack into his back.

Her lips crashed into his, and he spun her around in his exuberance. He barely heard the cheers of his mages over his pounding heart and Azalea's satisfied growls.

Open Doors, Open Hearts

As soon as the sun had risen, they had ridden hard to leave the suffocating stench of the burning Karden bodies behind. Three of the horses had been killed in the conflict, so Azalea offered hers up to ride behind Nilos. She kept one arm on his waist and the other on her sword hilt. Deidre rode in front of Jarrett, her partially healed arm in a rough sling. The blush on her cheeks and the slick smile on Jarrett's lips told Azalea that neither were particularly unhappy with the arrangement.

Something about the skirmish had shifted things between the group. The Zelarians no longer regarded her with cold side-eyed glances, and Azalea found she was not as distrusting of them as before.

Nilos had reached out to the guards at Sardit through an enchanted mirror, alerting them of what had occurred. Azalea had nearly demanded they alter their return trip where they learned that a neighboring village had barely survived a separate attack. The news that their forces were, indeed, gathering at Heirlight had solidified. The fierce soldiers of Tyldon combined with the magic of Zelarum had succeeded thus far in keeping them confined, but small groups continued to slip by the joined armies.

As the day grew on, they passed crowds of Zelarians on the main road. They parted before the group, issuing out cheers as their Prince galloped past, but a few had hurled insults at the sight of a Tyldonian knight in their midst. Azalea knew word of the wedding was still making its way throughout the land, and that there would be no small amount of gossip regarding his new, future Empress with the surrounding villages seeking refuge behind Sardit's massive walls.

Azalea clung tighter to her husband as the sun dipped lower. Flurries gusted around them, whipped on the biting wind. Just as the sun was touching the top of the mountains that trailed from the north down to the west, a tower came into view. Nilos had not been joking when he said the city was a fortress.

Massive stone walls, carved from the stalwart mountains that created an imposing backdrop behind the palace, loomed higher than trees of the forest they had broken free from. Mages in silver robes patrolled the ramparts, and the crimson sunset caught the threads of garment as if they were on fire.

A single gap broke the landscape of the mountains that curved to the north, creating an arch that was barely visible in the snow rushing threw it. Azalea knew what that was, had read stories of its dangerous river that fed the Northern Sea, the passage of the North Wind.

She drank it all in, memorizing the image before her as their weary horses pealed at the sight of home. Five, silver roofed towers spaced around the palace refracted the sunset onto the snow-capped peaks in the distance. It was not her golden palace high above the sea, but its beauty was born of a fairy story.

A mage riding to their left, Robin, passed Nilos his crown. Neither he nor Azalea had been wearing them on the ride. He slid it one handed onto his hair. As soon as his wife settled it onto his brow, a heralding of trumpets erupted. The people ahead on the road parted swiftly, cheering as they rode through. They did not give Azalea or Jarrett scathing looks, Nilos noted fondly. Word of their forest skirmish must have traveled to the streets of the city already. He braced his arm over Azalea's as Anurob sprinted through the main square and under the portcullis that separated the palace fairway from the city.

His horse came to a heaving stop at the steps leading up to the main door, and Nilos slid from his back and helped Azalea down. The doors blew open, and he half expected his mother to come sweeping out.

Instead, his Aunt Sylva led the staff down the snow dusted steps. In his and his mother's absence, she had been left in charge of palace affairs.

"Thank the Star Makers you are alive," she breathed, curtsying low before cupping his face. She turned her eyes on Azalea and gave another, shorter curtsy. "Your Highness." Then she turned to her daughter who was being helped off Jarrett's horse and began her fuss all over again.

"Deidre, your arm!"

Azalea was too exhausted to feed into the woman's chilled greeting. Her fingers and toes were numb, and her stiff joints ached at her weight.

A raven-haired woman dashed down the stairs, her rounded belly emphasized by her billowing robes, and grabbed Robin in a crushing hug. The mage, still sporting bandages of his own, accepted her kiss before dropping to his knees and pressing kisses against her pregnant belly.

"Let's get you fed and warmed," Nilos murmured to his wife. He wrapped an arm around her waist. "Captain Jarrett, you are to go to the guest wing and rest. I do not want to hear a word about it. You look dead on your feet." The man opened his mouth to protest, but Nilos raised a hand. "You cannot protect Azalea if you are exhausted. Now go."

He was spent and sore himself, but his bride swayed dangerously in his arms. After the energy he had expended the night before, Nilos knew a heavy meal and warm bath would have him unconscious for the rest of the night. "Hold on." He whispered to her, lifting her into his shaky arms. "Fatigue does not override tradition in Zelarum."

Azalea squeaked in surprise as she was swept off her feet and carried up the stone steps to the open doors. She was too drowsy and chilled to protest against his warm embrace. When they crossed the threshold, she had no energy to lift her head to take in the differences between their homes, except the imposing portrait over massive stone doors.

A man who bore a striking resemblance to her husband sat on a throne, but his portrait was shrouded in a thin, black veil. Beneath him, blue and silver candles burned in black sconces.

The portrait disappeared from view as her husband carried her up a sweeping, stone staircase, down a lamp-lit hall, to a pair of pale, wooden doors.

She leaned into his arms when he lowered her and ushered her inside.

A woman hurried in from an adjacent door, and Nilos found his energy temporarily renewed.

"Asha-anne." The older woman beamed back at him, not even bothering with protocol, and wrapped her arms around him in a tight hug. He welcomed her embrace, kissing her wrinkled cheek.

"Nilos! I was so worried," she hummed, rubbing his back

and kissing his cheek in return.

Nilos pulled back to cup the face of his childhood nursemaid.

"When I heard what happened, I was so terrified that you were hurt." Her keen, ebony eyes found his wife, who was shivering quite violently and attempting a smile.

"Asha-anne, may I present my wife, Princess Azalea." Nilos took Azalea's hand and helped her forward. "Azalea, this is Asha-anne. She was my nursemaid until I went away to the academy."

Azalea braced herself for the same, cold greeting the first woman had given her, but the older woman pulled her into a tight hug and kissed her messy hair. She tensed, reflexively, and pulled away.

"Nursemaid?" she chuckled through her wind-burned throat. "I have only been with him for four days, and he already tests my patience. I can only imagine what raising him must have been like."

"A handful, I will tell you that." Asha-anne fluttered her hands. "I will send dinner up to you immediately. You two must be exhausted." With one last smile, Azalea was once again alone in a bedroom with her husband.

"I need a bath to warm my bones." Azalea groaned. "I will be eternally grateful if someone has drawn us a hot bath already." She pulled at her heavy coat buttons and began stripping it off as Nilos shed his own lighter one and stepped through the door Asha-anne had entered from.

Nilos was not surprised to find his massive, stone bathing tub filled nearly to the brim. Asha-anne's floral magic still lingered in the air, mingled with the rich scent of minerals and fragrant oils drifting up with the steam. Her signature purple flames flickered in the niches of the tub's walls. Satisfied his wife would, indeed, be able to relax in the healing oils Asha-anne had mixed in, he returned to her.

His weary wife was perched on the sofa before the blazing hearth where he usually enjoyed reading. A soft smile pulled at his lips at the sight of her struggling with her boot laces. Despite the warmth of the fire, her shivers were as visible as the frustration scowling from her face.

"Let me," he chuckled, kneeling before Azalea. He plucked the laces loose and slid them from her feet. Her wool socks were soaked with cold sweat, and he peeled those away to reveal her red toes. Gingerly, he took each foot in his hand and massaged the blood back into them.

Azalea sighed at her husband's touch, leaning her head back against the cushion behind her.

"If you keep that up, Your Highness, I may fall asleep right here." His hands were magic but not the way she had experienced them in their secluded darkness. She was too spent to be ashamed of the husky groan that escaped her.

"I need to get your blood flowing before you get in the bath," he murmured. Under his touch, her numb feet pricked and tingled near to pain. "If you warm them too quickly, it may result in injury."

After a few more mesmerizing moments, Azalea accepted his proffered hand and followed him into another room. The same, rich, sultry oil that had wafted from him during the wedding teased her senses, accompanied by the unmistakable earthy lure of rosemary and the homey ting of sea salt.

"What is that fragrance?" Azalea purred as she tore at her clothes. The stone steps leading up to the rim of the pool were not inviting, but the promised relief the water offered was too much to deny.

"Moon lily." Nilos did his best not to stare at his wife's bare body as it was revealed so casually to him. "The flower of the Royal family."

He averted his eyes and knelt to remove his own boots. When he looked up again, Azalea was already settled in the water.

"Joining me?" she hummed, even as she rested her head back against the stone.

"If you do not object," he replied and promptly divested himself of his clothes.

Azalea stretched in the water, forcing her eyes not to close and tug her into sleep.

With blind experience, she undid her braid and fingered combed her waist length tresses free of tangles. Just as she had pushed the bulk of it under the water, the bath stirred. Glancing up, she found her husband sinking into the water, and his legs framed her own.

Azalea watched, bordering on delirium, his catlike muscles stretch and flex as he dipped a rag into a jar of white paste on the ledge beside them and begin to scrub his neck.

Her fingers twitched, oddly yearning to take the cloth and do it for him. Shaking herself, she grabbed the cloth closest to her and filled it with the same, gritty, soap paste. Closing her eyes, she cleansed herself of the stench of the road and battle.

Nilos chided himself every time his rebellious gaze drifted over the bath water to the goddess opposite him. Though the water covered most of her, her powerful yet graceful shoulders begged to be stroked and kissed. When she drew the cloth over her face, her breasts broke the surface, gifting him a brief vision of their bare fullness.

Even with the abrupt shift in their comfort levels, he did not think she would appreciate him leaning forward to take the cloth and clean her skin of everything but his touch. Azalea had made it clear. She would come to him when she was ready to join her pleasure to his.

"This should help with your hair." He offered her a bar of hair soap from the tray where it rested. His wolf paused in her fuss with the golden curtain floating around her. He reminded himself to thank Asha-anne for insuring that more than his usual soap scrub was ready for his bride. "The bottle, there, should be a lotion to soften it." He pointed to the lavender jar, and he smiled when a third bottle was revealed as he slid it towards her. A Tyldonian label proudly announced itself as hair oil. "And, a little taste of home for my wolf."

Azalea's dark rimmed eyes softened as she lifted the bottle, and her silent thanks was visible in the way she uncorked it and inhaled.

Azalea jerked when a knock broke her sudden jaunt through the rose gardens outside the Sun Temple. She sighed, reaching for a towel, but Nilos beat her to it.

"I will go. You stay here." His hand squeezed her knee under the water. "It is probably Asha with dinner."

Azalea hummed in consent and ducked her head under the water as he stood. She was not quite ready to see him fully bare, though she had felt him through clothes in their heated arguments. Once she was sure he was gone, she came up for air and began the soothing, familiar ritual of washing her hair and praying to the Sun Raisers for their glory upon her crown.

Nilos kissed Asha-anne's cheek when he found her and her grandson, Lyric, placing dinner trays upon the table in his sitting area. A few of the servants were placing the chests containing his and his bride's clothes near the closet door.

"Thank you for preparing things for Azalea," he said, as Asha-anne patted his cheek like he was no older than a boy. "I have not seen her smile as brightly as she did when she found the hair oil."

"I have been working to find more things to make her stay comfortable, but I did not have time to prepare much more than toiletries," replied the nursemaid. "With little Marcel going off to academy, I was afraid my services at the palace were coming to an end. Staying to help you make this a home for your wife is a blessing I hold in honor."

"She is difficult," he huffed, "be patient with her."

"Is she difficult?" asked Asha, "or is she a scared wolf trapped in a cage she never considered may close around her?"

The question hung in the air as Asha and Lyric shooed the servants from the room.

Scared? The word had not once crossed his mind. Angry? Yes. Grieving? Undoubtedly. Uncomfortable? Most definitely. But scared? He had yet to see fear upon Azalea's face. Though, he noted her behaviors in the forest when he covered her mouth were not dissimilar from a wolf trapped in a hunter's snare.

His heart twisted, and he dragged his hand down his face. How could he have missed something so obvious? Berating himself, he threw open one of her trunks and began to dig for something for her to sleep in.

A soft clearing of the throat drew his attention to the door to the bathing chamber.

The object of all his newest desires and confusion stood in nothing but a towel around her frame. He had yet to see her hair loose, but it hung around her in liquid gold, veiling part of her face and concealing her arms and shoulders.

For the first time in four days, the word delicate settled itself into the mosaic he had mentally crafted to describe his wife. She was far from fragile, but the soft flush along her cheeks and the gentle tuck of a wet lock behind her ear revealed the softness she so fiercely concealed behind her sharp tongue and sharper blade.

"That for me?" Azalea asked the starry-eyed man staring at her. Her favorite pair of winter sleeping pants and the matching, golden shirt that went with them were clutched in his hands.

"Um, yes." She had not seen his cheeks turn that particular color pink before, and she delighted in the way it spread up to the tips of his ears. He crossed to her holding the items out "I, um, also found your comb."

Azalea took her things, and she held back a giggle when he tugged at one ear while running his hand over his short, dark hair.

"I will be back after I dress." She shut the door without waiting, forcing her heart to stop its manic flutters at the open worship in her husband's eyes.

Though she had worn her consummation gown for him, Azalea was not quite ready to expose all of herself to his view. She knew she was beautiful, and she knew he found her so, but never had any man—barring Jarrett—ever looked at her like she was as soft and entrancing as the flower for which she was named. The few, confident men and women who had dared to pursue her at a festival or a ball had praised the beauty in her strength and combat, always allowing her to take the dominance in the fevered kissing and heavy petting.

Armored in the thick garments, Azalea squeezed the sun-rose oil into her hair and rejoined her husband in his chambers.

"Some days I really dislike the energy this requires," she

grumbled, working her comb through a particularly stubborn tangle at the end of her hair.

"Why do you not cut it then?" asked Nilos. "Many women in Zelarum cut their hair to their shoulders." He uncorked a bottle, and defiance snarled in her chest. "It would not detract from your beauty."

"It would be a disgrace," she explained, making an effort not to snap at him. "The longer a woman's hair, the longer she has been fighting and never conquered." Her husband paused in pouring the wine. "In Tyldon, a woman only cuts her hair if she is bested in true combat, if her spouse falls in battle, or if she loses a child during the battle of birthing." She resumed her combing. "To cut it is to grieve only the most devastating of losses or a disgrace to her honor. Did you study nothing of my people at those elaborate academies in Arcadius?"

"I did," sighed Nilos. "I knew this, but I spoke without thinking." He uncovered a tray before one of the chairs, and a succulent aroma drew her closer to the table. "You eat, sweet wolf, and I will comb it for you?" She peeked at the bowl waiting for her. "It is good, bacon and corn chowder. Trust me."

Trust him?

Two days ago, those words would have sent Azalea off on an internal tirade about why he was a pretentious, self-righteous coward. Now the words allowed her to extend the comb and settle into the chair.

Nilos worked the comb delicately through Azalea's soft hair as she ate. With each stroke through the damp strands, he watched her tense posture relax into the same, hesitant, softness as when she had first come from the bath. Though his own muscles protested even this easy task, he took the silence and the trust she offered him in that moment to ask what he suspected was true.

"Azalea?" he whispered, separating another section of her hair and untangling the strands at the end.

"Hmm?" came her soft reply around the spoon in her lips.

"Are you—" he paused, uncertain if he should approach it gently or directly. She preferred directly, he knew, but she was just as likely to respond with anger and retract the precious moment of allowing him to care for the visual symbol of her pride and honor. "Are you afraid? I mean, of being here in Zelarum, of being married to a man you did not meet until you stood at the altar?"

Her spoon clanked in the bowl, and her shoulders heaved with her heavy, audible, intake of breath.

"Am I afraid?" she whispered. He did not look up from his task, but the gulp of her wine spoke volumes. "I first drew blood on the battlefield at sixteen, supplementing Nirlas's battle against Krislion's invasion. It is also where I first felt what it was like to plunge my blade into a man and see the life leave his eyes."

Nilos did not speak, though he remembered his father working relentlessly to broker peace between the two nations across the western sea.

"I commanded my first battle at eighteen, when Krislion retaliated for our alliance during that war." Another gulp, another gentle sectioning of her hair. Nilos remained silent as he drank in the glimpse of what had made Azalea into the woman seated before him.

"I was wounded, fractured ribs from a kick by one of their generals," chuckled Azalea, dryly. "I was so afraid, because the pain was unbearable, but I knew what to do. I had trained, had prepared, had accounted for the possibility, and I tossed my shield aside, grasped my sword in both hands, and took his head at the gates of Horizon, my mother's childhood home."

Nilos took the final section into his fingers, savoring the silken waves, and treated them as gently as she offered her words.

"I have no training for this." Her whisper trembled, nearly cracking. "No army. No guard. What little strategy I had time to formulate before the wedding has been undone."

Nilos lowered her hair to her back, smoothing it neatly so each dip and twist aligned as precisely as possible.

Finally, she turned, and though she did not speak the words, the truth shaded her solemn gaze.

Azalea held her breath as her husband knelt before her. His blue eyes danced between hers, imploring her to trust him in ways she did not feel she could ever, truly, give.

"I know you are capable of defending yourself," he murmured, and his fingers were down soft as he stroked her hair from her eyes. "But this is not your cage. This is not a hunter's snare meant to force you into domestication or a grave. You are as free to live and thrive as any other woman in the empire."

"Would you feel the same, if it were Deidre married off and carted away to Dawncliff?"

Her husband's hand fell away, and he stepped back. Azalea nodded at his wordless answer and abandoned her half-eaten meal to cross to the bed. She paused only to open the curtains at the nearby window, before crawling under the heavy blankets and curling onto her side.

The view of the stars was blocked by the whirling wind of the snowstorm that had finally unleashed its fury. It shook the panes, and its raging beauty mirrored the renewed anguish in her core.

Azalea was caught in the little globe her father had once brought back from a trip to meet Emperor Rallios in Arcadius. It still sat alone on the shelf above her vanity where she left it.

If she quieted her thoughts, she could pretend she was there. Outside of that glass was her airy bedroom. The cooler, winter breeze would be bringing in the sound of gulls and waves. She simply had to reach out and push. The globe would tumble and smash on the floor to free her, and she could dash down the hall to find her family laughing as Alastrex showed off his newest acrobatic skills.

There was no silent man eating his lukewarm chowder across the room, only Jarrett pretending his leg was chopped off by Rex's wooden sword. No heavy door opened so the dinner tray could be placed in the hall, only her mother's Bloodsworn warrior, Evalmir, tossing grapes at her father's warrior, Gretchlia.

The soft curtains of the ladies' maids' quarters billowed out, catching on her fingers as Azalea found her girls giggling over a kitten who had snuck into the garden. The crisp mist of morning dew teased along her lashes as she lifted the dawn offering to the Sun Raisers from her balcony.

The sun was warm, so gentle upon her skin, as she lounged clothed only in the sky on the grass of Princess Cove, while Jarrett teased a likewise nude Lady Sharene with a slice of sunfruit. The ocean licked the sand below, beckoning the trio to dive into its waves.

Then, there was silence. Deafening, suffocating, crackling silence, and it jerked her from her useless fancies.

The storm was gone, revealing the fullest of moons in a frozen sky. Its silver light blinded her. She shot up, her heart pounding.

A warm arm wrapped around her waist, and warmer lips pressed into the back of her shoulder.

"It is only the first snow," came Nilos' husky, slurred whisper. "The quiet, that is. Lie back down and rest."

"I have never heard anything like it," whimpered Azalea, her heart desperate for the crashing roar of the sea. "My hearing feels odd, like ringing and buzzing all at once."

"We can get up and go look." Her husband shifted behind her, and another gentle, whisper of a kiss pressed into her hair. "If it will help you relax."

"I would rather stay warm," she admitted, turning to seek out the now familiar space on his chest. In truth, she needed to hear his heart, because the silence was not simply the snow. Her wolf had stopped howling for a pack that would never come. She silenced her own groan of complaint when her lower back and stomach twinged an all too familiar warning. She would have another month before anyone would question the stability of their wedded alliance.

Confessions and Confrontation

Azalea took advantage of her first week in Sardit to familiarize herself with the layout of Whitestar Palace and its grounds. She had faced some push back upon attempting to access the armory, but Deidre had been passing and swiftly reminded the sneering guard of what her newest cousin's status entailed.

Deidre was also the first person to volunteer when Azalea announced she would personally begin combat training for any who wished to attend just after dawn every morning. Although, given how Deidre always seemed to end up as Jarrett's sparring partner, she was beginning to suspect that the red-haired woman was there for an entirely different reason.

Azalea's routine was established so securely that she barely had time to wonder how she had fallen into it. Breakfast, morning pregnancy exam, training, court affairs, lunch, war council, Nilos' tutoring on imperial affairs, dinner, bathe, fail to seduce him into more than a gentle kiss, sleep. Round and round her life tumbled, as out of her control as it was clenched firmly in her fists.

By the fourteenth morning, the cycle Azalea found herself trapped in snapped something within her.

"Still no pregnancy," grunted Lady Sylva, as she lifted her bare hands from Azalea's stomach. The pine scent of her healing and nature magic rustled with the movement. "My nephew *is* finishing inside of you, is he not?"

"I know how to make a baby," growled Azalea, and she yanked the wraps of her dress back around her. "I cannot force his seed to take root." It was as close to the truth as she could manage, given that her husband had made no move to fulfill his promise of consummation.

It was not entirely his fault, either. The conversation from their first night echoed in her mind every time they were alone. He had also stopped rising to her antagonizations, refusing to handle or speak to her as he had in the forest and the tent. Despite sharing his bed every night, her husband did little more than hold her as they voiced their concerns over the latest news from the battle front.

"Perhaps you should stop training as intensely," said Deidre's mother. Her silver, chin length hair rustled as she shook her head. "The stress—"

"All women of able body in Tyldon train." Azalea jerked on the lighter cloak she wore to keep off the chill of the halls. "My mother carried and delivered two strong, healthy children, and my father's mother delivered seven." She yanked up the daggers she had abandoned on a nearby table for her morning exam and fitted them into their concealed pockets throughout her dress. "If training prevented conception, Tyldon would be a barren kingdom and not the most sought-after military in the world."

"You have given your body no time—"

"Have you considered, perhaps, it is your family's seed that is weak and not the soil in which it is being sewn!" Azalea ripped open the door. "You and your sister only managed a child apiece, and you lived your lives in the epitome of peace and relaxation." She stormed out before she could see her insult land.

"What was that about?" asked Jarrett, pushing away from the wall near the door.

"None of your business," she growled. "Follow me."

Without looking back, she prowled to her husband's chambers and traded her indoor slippers for her fur lined riding boots.

"Those are not sufficient for training," offered her knight, but Azalea simply yanked the thin, Zelarian coronet from her head and tossed it onto the bed. "Did someone replace the sugar in your breakfast porridge with bitterroot."

"No." Azalea ripped her thick riding cloak from its hook where it had hung, untouched, since her arrival and tossed her thinner one aside. Then she dug in the drawer of a side table and tugged out the cinched, leather pouch inside. She took in her knight's leather armor and shrugged. "Fetch your traveling cloak and meet me near the siege tunnel exit in five minutes."

"What for?" asked Jarrett, but Azalea blew past him and took hold of the ring that led from Nilos' tower room directly to her destination. She slipped inside before it could fully open and yanked the chain on the other side so that the narrow cabinet slid back into place.

She had barely made it to the dimly lit door that led into the edge of the city proper when Jarrett joined her. His own traveling cloak was fastened, concealing his sword.

"Where are we going?" he asked.

"Nilos told me that I am not being held prisoner," she scoffed, shoving up the metal bar that kept the door secure. "He told me this is not a cage, that I have all the rights and privileges of any woman in Zelarum."

"And we are running away because you are not a prisoner?" Jarrett held the bar as Azalea dug into the lock with her dagger.

"We are going to the market," she chuckled as the lock clicked. She concealed the dagger in her boot and pulled out her bag of fortune to jingle it. "On my husband's coin."

"You wicked little thief," laughed Jarrett.

"If I am his equal, then I share in his treasury," she retorted before pulling her hood up. She tugged the door open, peering around to make sure the alleyway along the wall Nilos' had shown her was empty. "Hurry." She creeped out, holding the door for Jarrett, and she yanked it shut as the siege bar slammed down.

She breathed in the metallic tang of the snowy air and looped her arm through Jarrett's.

"You have been to town more than I," said Azalea. "Lead the way."

The thrill of sneaking out had never ceased to liven her spirits, even home in Tyldon, and she reveled in the weight it lifted from her chest as she perused the market stalls and shops.

Despite the growing number of refugees, the citizens were all clean and in good spirits. The only hint of war that was visible were the increased guards on the ramparts and an ever-growing number of merchants selling weapons or spells for combat.

Apart from the gray sky, the flurries of snow, and the open displays of daily magic, Azalea could have been back at home in Tyldon. Even still, she kept close to Jarrett with her cloak tight to enjoy the breath of freedom she had stolen.

"I do not think I have seen you smile this much in almost a

month," said Jarrett, as she paused to peruse a glass case. Steam from the warm pastries inside fogged her view, but she spotted the tell-tale seeds of a sunfruit peeking from the filling of one.

"Is that a sunfruit pie?" she asked, mimicking the lilted bur many women of the court put on. Her mouth watered at the thought of the tart, sweet, cinnamon-like filling.

"Aye, mi'lady," chuckled the man behind the cart's small oven. "You must be from the Arcadius Academies to spot it that quick." It was not the first time that day her bad accent and sun-kissed skin had prompted the question.

"I am," lied Azalea. She dug out four silver coins and plopped them into his hand. "Double, because I know how difficult they must be to get fresh this far north."

"Thank you, mi'lady." The man passed her the pie, and she hummed when the warm, wax wrapper heated her palm. "They're too sour for my taste, much like the Tyldonian people as a whole."

Her wolf bristled, but Jarrett squeezed her arm in warning.

"If you knew her personality, you would know sour is not a problem for her," her knight chuckled and tugged her swiftly away.

Azalea savored the heated sticky explosion of home on her tongue. The baker had not quite balanced the sugar in the pie crust to true Tyldonian standard, but it was close enough that it made her close her eyes and briefly forget the snowflakes settling on her fingers. Her soul deep trust in Jarrett allowed her to follow his lead without breaking the vision of the Castlewood playing behind her eyelids.

A gloved thumb brushed her cheek beneath her hood, and she finally opened her eyes to find he had guided her into a little seating area outside of a tiny shop that smelled of chocolate and warm milk. Her vision was blurred, and she blinked rapidly before she realized it was tears and not melted snow.

"In eight years, I have seen you cry three times," murmured Jarrett. "When you were anointed your father's heir, when Rex had the pox, and at your wedding reception." Azalea licked the salty tears and the sticky remnants of the pie from her lips as she tried to steal back the moment of home. "This makes four."

"I miss home," she sighed. "Taste, and you will see." She offered him the pie, but he shook his head.

"No, this is more than that." His ochre eyes narrowed, raking over her face. "I know you, every emotion, every pain, every joy, and the last few days I have watched you close yourself off, even to me." Jarrett cupped her other cheek. "This is more than homesickness. I have humored this tryst into town, because I thought you would open up and confess what is troubling you."

"Leave it be, Jarrett," growled Azalea. She turned her face from his touch and tossed the remnants of her pie towards a tree where a flock of ravens perched. The warmth of home was lost.

"No, not this time." His fingers caught hers, anchoring her in place when she tried to lose herself in the passing crowd. "You said you wanted to prove you were not in a prison nor a cage."

Azalea regretted the snide comment she'd made in their escape.

"Has he hurt you, Azi?" The question came with the rumbling growl of his tiger stirring. "Behind closed doors, where I am not permitted to be, has he put his hands on you? His magic?"

"Of course not," she hissed. The idea was absurd. Nilos would not even bed her for fear of causing her pain, though she had made it abundantly clear she was willing and ready.

"You have been suppressing the wolf all morning." Jarrett pulled her closer, so their words could not be overheard. "You always chew your lip when you do. Why are you silencing her?"

"Lady Sylva blames me for not conceiving." Azalea spat the words, her wolf bristling at the accusation that still stung so deeply.

"The old witch needs to keep her pointed fingers to herself," snorted Jarrett. He kissed her brow and looped his arm through hers. Azalea relaxed as it seemed she had satisfied his suspicions. "I am certain your husband has no issue in attempting the process." Her knight chuckled. "Given the way he can go less than a few moments without staring at you like a man perceiving a goddess given form."

Azalea's cheeks burned, and she swallowed past her heart pounding in her throat.

"Tell me," teased her knight, tickling her ribs as they passed an oddities shop. "How fares his sword in the battle of pleasure?"

Azalea danced away from his fingers and pulled her hood lower over her face, using the excuse of observing a sign beneath a dagger displayed in the window.

"The blonde cook." Jarrett squeezed her shoulders and leaned in to peer over her shoulder. "Has nature magic, and his wife controls water. The things they can do..." Her knight hummed, and Azalea rolled her eyes. Of course he had already found companions to warm his bed. "Has Nilos used his magic on you for pleasure, yet? That lightning looks like it could be *intense*." Jarrett poked both her sides, laughing. "Is he as ravenous as the storms he wields?"

"I do not know!" Azalea snapped, whirling to face her friend. "He will not bed me." The broken groan escaped her lips before she could stop it, and she slapped her hand over her mouth.

Jarrett's eyes blew wide, and his hands fell to his sides.

"You have not—" her tiger lowered his voice, looking to make sure they were not overheard. "Azalea Solaria, you have not yet consummated your marriage?"

She shook her head, lowering her trembling hand as her soul-wolf whined at being found in her lie.

"But your wedding sheets and your gown, they were bloody." Jarrett's voice shook as he pointed a finger at her. "I saw them. I bore them to your parents and the Empress myself."

"He used his fingers," she breathed, seizing his wrist and pulling his hand down. "He refused to bed me. He said it felt as if he were raping me, and he would not tarnish himself or my heart with that pain."

"You must fix this, and you must fix this swiftly," snarled Jarrett. "If his aunt is already suspicious, the Tyldonian and Zelarian war councils may demand a chaperoned bedding." Her knight seized her arms, shaking her lightly. "Is that what you want?"

Azalea opened her mouth to answer, but a crack of thunder slammed down the road. Windows rattled. Birds scattered. Screams burst around them.

She turned, and the wolf spread into her arms and legs as she pulled her daggers from her dress. Beside her, Jarrett's sword flashed as he drew it.

Lightning shot from the silver roofs of the palace, and a thunderhead swirled up into the snow clouds, pushing them aside as it towered high. More thunder blasted down the street carrying on winds that ripped at their clothes. The thunderhead shifted, morphing into the shape of a howling wolf head.

"I believe you have been summoned." Jarrett sheathed his sword. "And if you know what's good for yourself and your people, you will use this opportunity to fix the violation of the alliance."

Six mages in guard robes marched towards them, their faces grim.

"Go play with your cook," snapped Azalea, as she tossed back her hood. "And none of you will lay a finger or a spell on me." She shoved past the guards and prowled up the road to the storm that raged within and above the castle.

Nilos cracked his knuckles after he signed the last petition for increased troops of the day.

The Kardens were slowly gaining more and more ground, forcing the conjoined armies back out of the mountains. Scouts had also reported seeing two cloaked figures at the highest point in the mountains, observing one of the fiercer battles. Their faces had been hidden, but one of them had blonde hair and wild blue eyes under his hood.

It had not been confirmed as Harvan, but Tyldonian troops had reported his hands glowed sickly white. His cousin's healing magic had glowed white his entire life, but it had twisted after the death of his mother. Nilos was convinced it was him, and he was certain, if Azalea had been present for the briefing, that she would have agreed.

His wife had not graced his presence since they parted after breakfast, but he knew she was devoted to training anyone willing in the art of physical combat. Given the increasingly distressing news from the front, she had undoubtedly lost track of time.

Still, her absence gave him a rare moment of solitude when the enchanted mirror over the hearth in his study glowed. The golden flecks of solar magic danced along its surface, and he grinned as he waved his hand.

"Mother." He stood, coming around his desk when the Empress's image came into focus.

"Nilos." His mother's voice was drained, and new wrinkles had formed in the corner of her eyes as she smiled. "How I have missed you." Her hands raised to the glass, her previously soft palms were red and rough.

"I missed you as well." Nilos squinted as he took in the other changes, smaller, things only a son would notice. A gray hair in her left eyebrow, silver strands forming at her temple, and small patches of healed pink skin on her neck. "You have been wounded."

"Minor injuries, I promise," she insisted. "I am quite safe. Our soldiers did not let the bulk of the fighters get close enough to do more than scald me."

"Where was the High General?" hissed Nilos.

"Piercing the eyes of two more with ice daggers," chuckled Idris. "He tended my wounds personally."

She waved her hand as if it were nothing, but the tension in her smile spoke the truth.

"We are on our second day of a lull in response, as they have retreated back into the mountains." His mother brushed her dark hair back from her face. "How is your new wife? I hope she finds our home accommodating." This smile was genuine. "I also hope you have been making her feel as at home and secure as you would a Zelarian bride."

Nilos flinched internally, guilt stabbing at how he had yet to fully confirm her—in marriage—as a citizen of their land. The guilt dug deeper, driven by the knowledge that he could not join his mother and fight for their people until he had seeded an heir in Azalea's womb. In the decision to not betray his soul nor his wife's emotional state, he was guilty of silent treason against his own nation.

"She is adjusting well." It was the closest he could reply without stepping into a lie. Idris had always been able to tell when he was untruthful, though he had never figured out what gave it away. "The cold is hardest for her, but she does not complain. She has taken over training anyone who wants to learn how to engage in weaponry." Nilos glanced towards the window. "She is usually here to discuss Zelarian affairs by now, but undoubtedly she has lost track of the time."

"I hope you and she are not at each other's throats," laughed Idris. "From what I have learned from King Brexten, she is as prone to a row as Deidre, if not more." His mother shook her head, ever the concerned parent. "Hopefully you are treating her with a bit more patience than you give yourself."

"Actually, we have not had any arguments since we arrived in Sardit." Nilos grinned and leaned back against his desk. "The wedding night and the first two days on the road, she was abrasive and shut off." He tugged at his ear, his cheeks burning as he recalled his part in her temperament. "After the Karden attack in the forest, she opened herself up to me more. I am unsure why, but I appreciate the glimpses of her softness she permits only me to see."

"She comes from a kingdom of warriors, Nilos." Idris chuckled and shook her head. "Seeing you in all the fury of the Stormwielder undoubtedly revealed that you are as capable of standing beside her in battle as a Tyldonian husband." A loud trumpet blast made them both jump, and the Empress frowned. "They are attacking." The mirror over the mantle went blank.

Nilos frowned, and he sent a swift prayer to the Star Makers to watch over her and their mages. Out of devotion to his wife, he sent a second to the Sun Raisers to likewise protect King Brexten and the warriors of Tyldon.

Resolving himself to the wait for the battle report, he turned his thoughts to the only thing that could ease his dread—sharing a meal with his wife.

"Robin!" he called wearily. His guard hustled into the room.

Robin avoided his gaze, wringing his hands, and, as the door shut, Nilos caught a glimpse of Juliett, Robin's wife, whisking past. Azalea had selected Juliett to be one of her ladies in waiting, despite the water mage's advanced pregnancy. "Was that Juliette coming to let me know Azalea is still down in the training fields and will not be joining me for my meal?"

"About that, Your Highness." Robin frowned, his healing earth magic glowing tawny as he did. "Juliett says the Princess never went down to training and neither did Captain Tiger-sword. Her handmaidens and ladies in waiting have been scouring the palace all morning, thinking she was sulking after her confrontation with your aunt this morning."

"Azalea is not in the palace?" Nilos shoved away from his desk, his stomach sinking to his feet. "Did you check with the guards at the thoroughfare portcullis?"

"And to the Northwoods," said Robin.

"What confrontation with my aunt?" snapped Nilos, as he pulled on his coat.

"From what a servant overheard whilst cleaning the chamber pots in your aunt's bathing room," said Robin, still avoiding his eyes. "Lady Sylva might have accused Princess Azalea of risking the possibility of conception by training."

Nilos whirled, the storm flashing dread and distaste at such an accusation from his mother's sister towards his future Empress.

"And Her Royal Highness might have insinuated that the fault lay in weakness passed from your mother into your seed." The skin along Robin's exposed neck caked with mud before crumbling to the floor. "She and Captain Tigersword were not seen after she left Lady Sylva's chambers."

Nilos' heart sank and twisted. Wherever his bride was, her anger or pain were entirely his fault. Thrice since her courses had passed she had attempted to seduce him, and thrice he had sent her to bed with a kiss to her brow because he knew her beckons came from duty and not desire.

"Lyric!" bellowed Nilos. "I know you are listening!" The door leading to the royal library on his left flew open. Asha-anne's grandson, a farseeing mage, scurried in. "Princess Azalea is missing. This is hers." He pulled the four strands of golden hair he had kept from the one and only time she had allowed him to comb her hair from his pocket. "Locate her and report back to me."

"Your Highness." Lyric took the hairs. "There is every possibility that the Princess simply went hunting. Grandmother said she asked two days past where the best—"

Nilos cut him off with a glare. He knew the teen was trying to calm him, but his mind ran wild with the possibilities of what the argument with his aunt may have driven her to do.

Then I shall send for Jarrett. The calm, decisive threat from their wedding night spun round in his mind. *If you will not perform, he is duty bound to do so in order to maintain my honor. He will never betray our secret.*

"Your Highness?" asked Lyric, gingerly.

"Well then check the forests!" exclaimed Nilos.

The storm of dread brewing in his chest tinged green with a cyclone. Lightning sparked from his hair and crackled from his fists as he clenched them. The thought of Azalea beneath or astride her knight brought a sickened anger he had no label for. Though he knew it would never be out of romantic love on her part, it scraped at his heart and his pride.

"My Prince, we should check the city first," said Robin, foolishly blocking Nilos' path to the door. "Perhaps she went into town. Juliett said her dress from this morning was not discarded in either yours or her chambers." Robin did not move from his space, though Nilos paused inches from his chest. "Princess Azalea would not go hunting in a dress."

"I do not care where you begin your search!" thundered Nilos as he shoved past his guard. "I told you to find her. Search every house in the blasted city if you have to. I will ride out into the forest on my own if you are all too cowardly to join me!"

He knew it was not his guards' fault Azalea had slipped past them. Prince Alastrex had warned him before the wedding that she was apt to sneaking out without an escort. Yet, there were too many possibilities to not fear or dread. What if she did sneak out with the Captain to hunt and encountered a wyrebear? Perhaps her growing affections towards him were falsities, and she had decided to return to join her father on the battlefield and risk the alliance by informing their families of their wedding night charade? What if, at that moment, Jarrett was clutching her bare body to his in some darkened tavern room to protect his Princess's honor from the judgement Nilos' own strict code risked besmirching?

With a wave of his arms, the doors blew open with a surge of wind.

It whipped around him, as the third possibility took the forefront of his mind.

Jealousy, that was the green clouds spinning in his chest. He named it, and he spited himself for it. Still, he could not be rid of the visions in his mind. Azalea's teeth pulled at Jarrett's bare shoulder, her nails scraping bloody welts into the tiger's back, their breaths and sweat mingling as their bodies moved, and it was her knight's name in her howl as she reached the pinnacle of her pleasure and waltzed in the starry sky.

Static of lightning tunneled his vision, and his panic and envy drove him to turn down the stairs. His own wind carried him, ripping at the candles and torches lighting the passages, until he hurled them at the doors to the heart of his castle.

The few people mingling in the throne room shouted when Nilos hovered past him, but he did not care.

"Get out!" he bellowed, swirling in his own vortex as he came to the steps of the royal dais.

They scattered, abandoning their cleaning supplies as they went.

"Azalea Solaria!" raged Nilos, tossing his hands into the air. "Heed my call!" His blood burned, sparking in his veins as he poured his fear and his jealousy into the air beyond the castle. Lightning danced from the metal adornments on the wall, and, in his mind, he saw it shoot from the roofs of the towers. "Attend to me, wife!" he commanded, molding the clouds into a message no person in town could misunderstand. Lighting crashed from the eyes of the wolf-head cloud, and he tossed its muzzle back, howling a tempest towards the forest and the city.

"If you want to test me," he snarled, willing another blast of wind in the trail of the first. "Then face me and test me!"

If his bride needed him to show his might, then he would show her. He had spent his life caging it away to prevent it from destroying the innocent as well as the guilty.

"I am Stormwielder!" roared Nilos. "As my grandmother before me!" He let loose another volley of lethal lightning, sending it striking from the towers to the grounds below and the sky above. "I, alone, command the sky to my will. I, alone, bend the fire of gods to my fists."

Around him, the tapestries whipped, and the walls trembled beneath the never-ending onslaught of his thunder.

"The rains bow to me!" He released another blast of wind, searching, seeking, finding the taste of wolf stalking against its might. "The clouds obey my every order!" Nilos knew it would drain him, once he allowed himself to rest, and he drew the energy of his lightning back to his soul to sustain him. Releasing it in a fury fueled by the thought of losing the wolf who had captured and consumed his heart, he bellowed out to his wife. "Come to me, *now!*"

The doors to the throne room slammed open, and silver pierced the hurricane of his rage.

Snarling, he struck the dagger with a bolt of lightning, sending it, and the other three that followed, hurtling into the wall.

"How dare you summon me like this!" screamed Azalea. His guards seized her arms. "You pompous, self-righteous, traitorous, feckless prat!"

"Release her and get out!" boomed Nilos.

Captain Shara barely avoided the dagger Azalea had produced from her sleeve, and Nilos zapped it from the Princess's hand as the guards fled the room.

"Lock us in!" he commanded and flew towards the feral-eyed wolf who was dashing towards him, her blade and bared teeth shining.

"I hate you!" howled Azalea, and Nilos slammed into her. He seized her wrists, rushing on his winds, until he had pinned her against the wall beneath a storm-tattered tapestry.

"Where were you?" he demanded, hissing as she jerked her wrist free. The dagger grazed his jaw. The shallow slice burned, but he sent lightning to her fingers. She yowled, dropping it, and her arm spasmed in his grasp when he pinned it to the stones.

"Why do you care?" Azalea spat, literally, as she growled and lunged for his neck.

"Answer the question!" Nilos pressed her tighter into the stones, pinning her kicking legs in place with his winds. "Where were you?"

"Why does it matter?" she snarled, and another glob of spit struck his brow.

"Did you let him take you to bed?" hissed Nilos, and he pressed his nose to her neck, seeking out any hint of her knight upon her skin. "If I lift your skirt, will I find Jarrett coating your thighs?"

"How very *dare* you?" Pain blazed in his cheek as Azalea

bit down and ripped at her dagger cut with her teeth. She promptly spit the blood at his mouth. "How dare you accuse *me!*"

Nilos squeezed her wrists, wrapping her body in tiny whirlwinds as she snarled and twisted between him and the wall.

"Where do *you* go when I fall asleep?" raged his Princess, her lips spotted with his blood. "Who are *you* filling that keeps your cockles too empty for your wife?" He blew the bloody spittle she hurled from her tongue to the side. "Which of the servants or ladies laugh behind my back every morning when *your* aunt reports to the court that *I* am still failing at producing an heir?"

"There is only you," swore Nilos, and his words cracked in a cacophony that rattled even his bones. "There will only ever be you. I love you, you hateful little wolf!"

"If you loved me, then you would bed me!" she screeched, and tears burst from her furious eyes. "Why will you not have me? Why do you refuse to take what is yours to take? If you love me, why do you disgrace me before your family?"

"Because I do not want to hurt you!" he thundered.

"How can you hurt me when I crave your body against mine?" sobbed his wolf. "Inside of me, around me, above me, below me. I want it all. I want you."

Nilos had no time to respond before she let loose a strained whimper and broke through the force of his magic to press her body to his.

"You have subdued me in combat," gasped Azalea. "That was all I ever needed. I had to know you could defend my people and my children should I ever fall in battle." More tears soaked her cheeks as she brushed her lips against his. "I am yours, always and eternally. By the blessings of the Sun Raisers, the wolf yields to her mate." His rage broke like clouds scattered by the dawn that lit his heart when she caught his lower lip in a gentle bite. "Make love to me, Stormwielder. Make love to me and sanctify our marriage before the gods."

A Sanctified Union

Azalea squealed when her husband whirled her away from the wall, hoisting her up by her hips. She clung to his arms and sighed when he caught the tender space beneath her ear in a firm bite.

"Sanctify it before the gods?" Nilos' voice graveled with promises that ignited fire between her thighs. "Is that what you want, my love?"

"Yes," she pleaded, pulling her neck from his lips to chase his kiss.

He bunched her dress, hefting her higher, until she could wrap her legs around him. She giggled and fumbled to untie the knotted strings at the collar of his shirt. Then, without warning, he dropped her onto a table. Her stomach lilted, because there were no tables this close to the thrones, and the hard surface could only mean one place.

"The altar?" Azalea hummed.

Nilos ripped the gold chain holding her cloak at her throat, lightning sparking behind his pupils as he smirked. Her Prince replied by kissing her roughly.

Azalea ripped at the buttons of his coat, shoving it open so she could claw his shirt free of his trousers. He growled and tore at the folds of her dress, and she squeaked into his tongue when he pulled back and stared at the finger length dagger she had tucked into the cleavage sheath of her bodice beneath.

"Undressing you is a hazard," snorted Nilos, "But worth all of the dangers."

Azalea's breath caught when he trailed the tip of the blade over her chest, tiny branches of his magic dancing out to bite deliciously along what was exposed of her breasts.

"You make the most lovely noises when I do that." Snickering he lowered it to the laces holding the bodice closed. "I wonder what noises you will make when I do this." For one horrifying moment, the wolf broke free of her lust in panic at the blade above her sternum, but Nilos jerked the dagger through the first few laces.

"Gods, Nilos," groaned Azalea, and she tossed her head back, gripping the edge of the altar as he cut through the remainder. "I think I may go mad if you do not *touch* me."

"Oh?" His voice was as slick as the smirk she knew he was wearing when the blade scratched along her sternum and pushed the bodice to the side. "The sweetest spoils of war are claimed slowly, with precision and keen study." She shivered as the cool air broke over her skin, trailing in the wake of the shower of sparks that popped and crackled pleasure into her core. "See how you flush, my sweet flower."

"Nilos," she pleaded, but she was rewarded with a sharper, quicker, spark of his storm against both of her pebbled nipples. "Gods! Yes!" She snapped her head forward, about to yank him deeper into the space between her thighs, when Nilos' lips closed around her right breast with a heavy suck. "By the stars," she crooned. She could not touch him with her dress and bodice half down her arms, so she shook them free and scraped her nails through the static sparking from his short hair.

She barely heard the dagger clatter to the floor before his hand cupped her other breast at the same moment his tongue swirled a spell against her tingling flesh.

Azalea clung to her husband, and she yipped out her delight when his palm heated in a flash of static that zinged sharply through her nipple and exploded low in her spine.

"Oh, again, please." She was rewarded with simultaneous, teasing shocks from his tongue and fingers, and Azalea dug her nails into his side as she mewled her approval.

Her husband released her with a wet pop, his eyes dark and heavy.

"I want you bare, now," demanded Nilos. He did not give his wife time to move, seizing the piles of material about her hip. "Lift." As soon as she was clear of the silver altar cloth, Nilos tugged her dress—and the fleece lined leggings beneath—down, hissing as they reached her riding boots.

"Blast." Nilos reached for the strings, but she batted him away.

"Take off your clothes, or I shall tear them off, husband," demanded Azalea as she ripped at her own laces.

Nilos wasted no time stripping himself down, oblivious to anything but the desire to satisfy every need she had ever, and would ever, lay before him. When he finally turned his attention back to his lover, he groaned aloud at the blessing before him.

"This altar has never held an offering as precious or divine as you," praised Nilos, as he stroked the satin skin of her gracefully powerful thighs up to her hips. "Though I am not a god, I do not think they would take offense if I allowed myself to feast upon you in worship."

"Pillow talk is unnecessary, darling," hummed Azalea as she arched her waist into his touch. "Cease your teasing and—"

Nilos hauled her to the edge of the altar, cutting off her seductive demand. Grinning at the giggled squeal his love gave, he dropped to his knees and pulled her legs over his shoulders.

"I seem to recall that the knowledge that I could snap you neck like this arouses you." Azalea's eyes flashed feral yellow when she tightened her knees around his head.

"Beyond measure." Nilos caught her supple thigh between his teeth and tugged. His wife fell back to her elbows, whimpering. "But, if you do, you will rob yourself of all the delights I have been yearning to gift you."

Without waiting for her retort, he pressed a kiss to the golden hair that crowned the apex of her thighs. Azalea's nectar soaked his lips, tart but succulent, like the scent of sunfruit freshly peeled.

"Let me hear you," he whispered, "Let them all hear you." Nilos chased the source of her taste with his tongue, finding her center drenched and heated. He groaned as she arched into his lips, her fingers scraping along his arms where he held her steady.

"Gods, Nilos!" Azalea's body hummed as her husband's tongue swirled and teased against her. Her soul-wolf basked in the adoration of her mate, preening and glowing in how he feasted upon her.

Digging her heels into his back, Azalea rocked her hips closer, crying out when his tongue thrust inside of her and curled. Stars danced across her vision, blotting out the carved statues that loomed over the altar.

The noises her husband made were a man starved, and

she voiced her protest as the swirling thrusts of his tongue vanished. Her complaints lilted into a sharp howl when Nilos caught the hooded bud only she had ever touched between his lips in a growled suck.

"Yes!" crooned Azalea, scratching his head to hold him in place. "There, more!"

She felt him smile against her, and his tongue lit sparks up her spine to burst behind her closed eyes. Then, his fingers dropped from her left hip. Keening, Azalea took advantage of the loosened grip to press her body firmer against his tongue. Her pleasure doubled, rolling through her like waves upon the rocks, when his finger thrust into her—curling as his tongue had—to stroke in time to the greedy dance of his licks.

"By Lyastra's fount," cried Azalea, praising and thanking the goddess of fertility and marriage for her husband's ravenous attentions.

She could not think, could not find a sliver of her careful control as she surrendered herself to the pleasure her Stormwielder lavished upon her. Another finger joined, stretching her deliciously, stroking sounds from her core she had never dreamed of allowing anyone else to hear.

She lifted her head, the world spinning drunkenly about her, to find his blue irises sparking magic up from between her thighs. His left brow lifted, belying the smirk as his fingers pressed deep and the tip of his tongue flicked against her with a wet crackle, and Azalea howled as the small bolts of lighting connected between them, buzzing deep within her and spiraling out.

"Again!" she pleaded, falling back and clutching the altar cloth in her fists. "Again, please, gods, Nilos!"

Another shock lit the sting of pleasure inside of her, and low in her thighs and core, the coil of release tightened. Azalea keened—wordlessly, gasping for air—trying to fight it back so she could savor her lover's touch longer, but Nilos was relentless in his passions.

The ocean roared in her ears, as her body tensed in its ecstasy. His venerations drove her higher. Again, his fingers beckoned within her, stroking praise in synchrony to the love of his lips and tongue. His magic sparked, snapping the coil within her, and Azalea howled as she tumbled from the precipice into a storm of stars.

Nilos released his lover from his lips with a wet pop, chuckling while she writhed upon the altar in a babbled mess of howls and whimpers. He licked her nectar from his lips and teased the pleasure swollen bud with another brush. Azalea cried out, shuddering before him, and he slowed his drenched fingers within her.

"You are perfection incarnate, my love," he praised and pressed a kiss to her trembling legs. "I could feast solely upon your taste for the rest of my days and spend an eternity listening to the song of your pleasure."

He eased her legs from his shoulders, pulling them around his hips as he stood.

Azalea's intoxicating eyes fluttered open, shining with the same giggles that broke from her petal-like lips.

"A poet and a prince." Her legs tightened against his waist, drawing him closer.

Nilos took himself in hand, trailing the head of his arousal through the flood between her thighs, and he squeezed her hip when she wriggled beneath him. Finding the epicenter of her pleasure, he paused until her gaze met his.

"I am yours," whispered Azalea, and Nilos sank into her

perfect, welcoming, embrace.

"Gods, you are divine," he groaned. She clung to his arms and lifted her hips to meet his thrust.

"You are glorious," crooned Azalea. "Kiss me, Nilos."

Nilos dropped his hands to the altar, catching his love's lips with a moan as he found his pace. Azalea's arms wrapped around him, her nails trailing stinging pleasure against his back. His wife sang her delight into his tongue.

He needed to feel her come undone around him, to witness her wild in her passion. His lover deserved nothing less than to be utterly inebriated with bliss.

Grunting at the aftershocks of her release fluttering around him, stroking pleasure unlike any he'd felt into his soul, Nilos slid his hand along her body until he found his treasure.

"Yes," whimpered Azalea, her teeth scraping his lip. "With your magic. Gods, the sensations are indescribable."

"Bite me," he commanded and caught the sensitive bud with a gentle shock between his fingers.

Burning pleasure raced down his spine as Azalea's teeth dug into his shoulder and her nails clawed trenches into his back. Thunder boomed above them, but he paid it no heed as he lost himself in his wife's adoration.

Nilos chased her release, biting the delicate skin of her neck and breasts with his lightning as Azalea marked her possession of his heart into whatever part of his heated skin her teeth and hands could touch.

The world faded to nothing, only her voice, her cries of his name, and their bodies joined in passion.

She tightened around him, fluttering, whimpering as he stroked another swirl of lighting against her in time to his thrusts.

"Howl!" cried Nilos, and his Princess released his burning shoulder to toss her head back.

Azalea lifted beneath him, her howl of completion rising and falling as it echoed with the thunder building in his core.

The storm chased his wolf over the edge, burying himself deep within her golden glow and releasing the tempest in his chest as he cried her name into her throat. The dam within him ruptured, and he held her hips tight to him as his own release spilled its completion within her.

Nilos needed her closer, impossibly closer, and he scooped his beloved into his arms to sink to the floor and silence her howl with his lips.

She rolled her hips against him, panting as their tongues met in desperate brushes, until she stilled in his embrace and buried her face in his scalding neck.

Their hearts beat wildly against each other, and Nilos stroked his trembling goddess softly as she whimpered and shivered.

He hissed as he felt himself softening, slipping from her, but he paid no heed to the hot trickle of their mixed releases when it dripped onto his skin.

Azalea licked the red marks she had left on her husband's shoulder tenderly, smiling at the way he shuddered and gasped. Tiny bells rang in her ears until the tossing seas in her thoughts grew peaceful and quiet, and she found herself mimicking the soothing strokes he teased along her back.

"That was more than I ever expected," she whispered, kissing the purpled indentions of her bite on his neck. A rogue burst of pleasure burst within her, making her tremble, and Nilos kissed her temple. Another trickle of his release seeped from her, making her hum. "I did not anticipate how much I would enjoy feeling your completion spilling from inside me."

"I was an impossible fool for denying us this," he murmured, "For thinking you would find no pleasure or peace in my love for you."

"Hush," huffed Azalea, lifting her lips from his skin to rest her brow against his. "I do not think either of us could have found pleasure this profound if it had not happened as it did." She kissed the tip of his proud nose, and she smiled when he kissed her chin. "I am, however, sorry I gave you any reason to doubt my fidelity to our vows or to you."

She pulled back to search his face for any further doubt or hint of suspicion that she would ever betray his honor or her own.

"My jealousy was ill placed and a direct response to my own, perceived failings," sighed Nilos. Azalea nipped his lower lip.

"Honor is not a failing." She kissed him gently, smiling as his powerful arms tightened around her. "I am sorry I questioned your honor of our vows."

"It was a reasonable reaction to my pointless accusations," replied Nilos, "I hope you no longer feel the need to sneak out instead of speaking with me when something has upset you."

"But if I no longer sneak out," teased Azalea, "Then what reason would you have to send a storm to summon me to your side." She was rewarded with a sharp smack of her rear, and she giggled at the sting. "Very well, Your Highness, I shall no longer sneak out *unless* I wish to quarrel with you until you bind me with your storm and make me beg for you to conquer my body."

"You are utterly incorrigible," growled Nilos, "But I would not love you as fiercely if you did not test the very edges of my thin patience." Again, his words struck something within her, nearly quenching the bliss that sang in her veins from their coupling. "I love you Azalea Golden Wolf."

She swallowed, trying to summon the words, but they choked in her throat as he kissed her.

"Do you not love me?" whispered Nilos, and his eyes tightened as they flicked between hers.

"I adore you." She cupped his cheeks, stroking them with her thumb as she pressed her chest into his. "Nilos, I adore you. I feel safe with you. I want to love you so badly it burns within my heart like wildfire."

"But you do not love me." His voice was raspy, and his tight grip that held her so wondrously loosened. "Was there another, back in your home, that I took you from?"

"No!" yelped Azalea, and she kissed him to reassure her husband of his sole claim to her affections. "There is only you, Nilos. I swear it upon everything. I am falling in love with you, but I have not yet reached the depths of that affection."

"Time, then?" His smile returned, crinkling his eyes as his embrace pulled her impossibly closer. "It is easy to forget, when you are this open and soft, that you have commanded battles and need more than promises and touches to earn the treasures of your affections."

"I will love you, Nilos Whitestar." Azalea rested her head against his shoulder, breathing in the scent of her perfume on his skin. "If you continue to challenge me and comfort me. A wolf's love is not easily won, but its loyalty is unwavering and immovable."

A knock echoed through the room, and she growled at the audacity of anyone to dare intrude upon their intimacy.

"One moment!" shouted Nilos, and Azalea grumbled as he untangled her from his embrace to wrap her in his coat and her cloak. She huffed, crossing her arms to conceal herself while he tugged on his trousers.

"Enter!" she snapped, and the door cracked. A familiar smile peeked around the edge. "What do you want, Jarrett?"

"If the two of you are finished scandalizing the entirety of the palace," chuckled her knight, "The guards need Prince Nilos on the main grounds."

"What for?" grunted Nilos, as he pulled on his shirt.

"Your lightning shattered a portion of the western wall when you summoned the Princess." Jarrett looked back over his shoulder, and a muffled whisper followed. Snorting, he turned his attention to them again. "Also, the wind destroyed the roof of the western barracks."

Azalea giggled, and he whipped his head to find her covering her mouth with his coat sleeve. Nilos winked at her, earning himself another burst of sweet laughter.

"I will be with them shortly." He waved the knight in after Jarrett spoke over his shoulder to whoever waited beyond.

"Is there something I may help you with, Your Highness?" asked the knight, as his dark gaze flicked knowingly between them.

"There is a hidden passage behind the statue of the Night Stallion." Nilos jabbed his finger at the rearing horse set in the corner of the northern wall. "It will take you to the siege tunnel. From there, escort my giggling, mess of a wife up to our room where she can dress without the entirety of the palace seeing her in such a state."

"As you wish." Jarrett bowed at the waist.

"Also," began Nilos, and he drew a heavy breath. "I accused Azalea of violating the vows of her marriage with you, and it was foolish of me to have done so. I have apologized to her, and she has forgiven me. It is only right that I apologize to you as well. I am sorry." He extended his hand.

"There is nothing to be forgiven," said Jarrett. The knight clasped his forearm and shook. "I am simply relieved to see her in better spirits than she was this morning. The blush of a happy marriage on her cheeks is a far sight better than tears that were on them this morning."

Nilos broke their grip to take Azalea's chin in his fingers and kiss her softly.

"I strongly agree, Captain," he murmured.

"If I might advise you, Your Highness," said Jarrett, and Nilos turned to him. "Disarm her *before* you pin her down if you do not want another cut cheek." The knight nodded towards Nilos' left cheek.

Nilos winced as he touched the forgotten scratch, and he chuckled.

"I will keep that in mind." He kissed his wife again, stifling her never ending fit of giggles, before clapping the man on the shoulder. "I will join you for dinner, sweet wolf."

"Do not keep me waiting," whispered Azalea.

Nilos stroked the red marks along her throat and neck where he'd returned her fierce affections.

"Do not cover these up," Her amber eyes blew wide, and her giggles faded. "That is an order, little wolf."

"Of course, my Prince," growled his sweet lover.

Nilos turned away, licking the remnants of her flavor from his lips as he strode towards the doors.

"So," he heard Jarrett whisper, "it sounded like you were enjoying yourself."

Nilos swallowed his chuckle at the light slap that echoed behind him.

"She was!" he called over his shoulder before opening the

door. "And she will again later tonight!"

Azalea glowered up at her knight as he rubbed his cheek and smirked.

Her husband's parting words burned promise in her core as she tightened Nilos' coat and her own cloak around her.

"How was his magic?" Jarrett scooped up her dress and daggers, and she rolled her eyes at him.

"You would like to know," she teased. Touching the tender places on her neck, she bit her lip and savored the way they bruised beneath her touch. "He is insatiable, and I have never felt so conquered and so worshiped as I do in his arms."

"Hang on." Jarrett's snort jerked her eyes open. He was staring pointedly at the wet spot on the silver cloth across the altar. "Did he consummate the marriage on the altar?"

"He took my asking him to sanctify our marriage before the gods quite literally," she giggled. In their many years of friendship, Azalea had not seen Jarrett look so impressed.

Questions Answered

Failure dug its claws into Azalea's chest when she awoke to the stain of her menses on the sheets of their bed. Despite sharing pleasures with her husband multiple times a day for weeks, their couplings had failed to secure him an heir.

It was not failure of her own body that drove her to irritation as she glowered out at the raging wind and ice of the first proper blizzard of the season, but in failing to succeed in the only battlefront she had been assigned to command. If she could not be at the head of the armies, battering back the terrifying increase of Karden forces, then she needed to come out victorious in the battlefield of childbearing politics. It was the only way her husband would be able to ride out and join with both of their armies.

His relief, she found, only served to irritate her more.

"I do no wish to ride out unless you are by my side," whispered Nilos. His hands were warm against her shoulders as he rubbed them.

"If you do not wish me to bite you," warned Azalea, "I would advise removing your hands from my body."

"You must stop seeing this as a duty." Nilos's hands dropped, but his lips pressed warmly to the top of her head. "You must be gentler with yourself, beloved. When you are meant to conceive, you will conceive. Until then, we have battles we can wage with the mind and the pen." Another kiss brushed her hair, and she turned away from him. "I know you despise being confined to the palace, but storms this early rarely last long. It should abate by sundown, and you will be free to trudge through the snow and take your irritation out on whatever guard is foolish enough to train with you.

She felt him move away, his robes brushing against the back of her skirts.

"Your Highnesses," said Lady Sylva. Azalea turned, finding the woman's face shimmering out from the enchanted mirror over the hearth of the war room. "The Empress and General Beakpoint wish to speak with you."

"Send them through," snapped Azalea. She did not want to look at the woman's face a moment longer than necessary. It had only taken her aunt-in-law half an hour that morning to ensure that everyone knew she, again, had failed to conceive.

Leaning against the wall, she drew her dagger and soothed herself with the repetitive dance of the blade over and under her fingers and palm.

Nilos paused beneath the looming portrait of his father, his face narrowed tight as they awaited his mother and her father's highest general. Azalea had not noticed the similarities between her husband and her deceased father-in-law until that moment. The late Emperor's jaw, cheeks, distinctive ears, and proud nose lived on in his son—as did the sharp, glacial blue of his eyes.

"Mother," said Nilos, but Azalea could not tear her eyes away from the portrait of Rallios as her husband moved towards the mirror. "General."

"It is good to see you well, darling," said Idris, but the wolf in Azalea's soul was too focused on Rallios' sightless eyes to give the Empress attention. "Azalea, I hope my son is treating you well."

Azalea did not answer, inching closer to the portrait, and tried to understand what her wolf saw that she missed. It was something important, something crucial in the Emperor's stern gaze.

"Azalea is not feeling well this morning," replied Nilos. "The blizzard that blew in yesterday has not abated, and her courses came this morning."

"Still no heir, then," grunted General Beakpoint. Azalea would have shouted at her to come produce an heir if she thought it were so simple, but the connections weaving in her mind were too critical to be distracted. "Princess, conception should be the focus of your attentions."

"I assure you that my wife has made conceiving an heir her utmost priority, General," growled Nilos. The low rumble of his thunder passed over Azalea without stirring her. "And I grow weary of people placing the sole weight of her empty womb upon her shoulders as if I am not equally responsible for fulfilling that duty to the alliance."

It was something in the eyes, something about Rallios' cold, unyielding eyes.

"Peace, Nilos," sighed the Empress, "I assure you that General Beakpoint was not implying it is solely Azalea's responsibility. It is just that, with what we learned this morning, it has never been more urgent for you to join our fight."

"What did you learn?" asked Nilos, and Azalea's neck ached as she stared up at the portrait above her face.

"Harvan is, indeed, in league with the leader of the Kardens."

General Beakpoint's voice was tight. "A monstrosity named Vadros. The creature should not even be alive."

"None of them should be alive," scoffed Nilos, "but why specifically is Vadros' existence more monstrous than the rest."

"Vadros was and remains the only mage born with the powers of necromancy," said Idris.

The word pierced Azalea's observations, anchoring her scattered threads of thought to hidden pieces of the unseen puzzle.

"From what the historians of both of our countries can understand," continued the General, "He was the son of a priestess of Estella and a priest of Solarus. Marriages between our nations were quite common along the borderlands, but rarely between the religious groups. After the Abysmal War, the tension between our crowns made it impossible for even those on the borders to intermarry."

"Yes, I know this, but how did Vadros ally himself with Harvan?" asked Nilos, and Azalea's tapestry of thought knitted together in the shape of Rallios' furrowed brow.

"We do not know," said Idris, "but we do know that Vadros is the one who started the first war. From what has been translated, he killed both of his parents for reasons unknown, raided multiple graveyards, and disappeared into what used to be the swamp-lands that would eventually become the wastes of Vanar."

"When he returned, he had an army of monsters he called Kardens and waged war upon both nations," said the General.

"It does not make sense," muttered Azalea, as she tugged and pulled with the wolf to tighten the tapestry weaving itself in her thoughts.

Nilos turned to his previously silent wife, biting back a

chuckle at the tip of the dagger tapping her lips. Her stare was glued to his father's portrait, as if his ghost would possess it and whisper the answers to whatever question furrowed her brow.

"What does not make sense, beloved?"

He approached her, pulling her dagger from her lips and kissing away the droplet of blood that beaded on the corner of her mouth.

He ignored the raised eyebrow of the Tyldonian general in the corner of his eye, but the warmth of his mother's sudden smile washed over him.

"What are you seeing that we are missing?" He turned her from the portrait by her chin, trying to make sense of the thoughts that whirled behind her tight expression. His wife kissed his cheek and brushed past him to prowl towards the mirror.

"Harvan is a healing mage, correct Your Majesty?" she asked, her dagger twirling between her fingers in the familiar pattern that bespoke her focus was about to stagger the room with something they'd overlooked.

"Yes, my husband's nephew was one of the most talented healers of this generation," his mother replied, and Nilos grinned at her as he followed behind his wife to join her at the mirror.

"Was his mother or father Rallios' sibling?" she asked, the dagger twirling faster.

"My uncle Xastran was Father's younger brother by two years," replied Nilos. He could not discern where his wolf was trodding, but he trusted her instincts would not lead to weightless claims. "He was an earth mage, like my father, and he died trying to stave off a flood near the village of Frostlake when I was four. Harvan was still on the breast at the time."

"So Harvan was raised by his mother here in the palace until he went away to the Academies?" Azalea rested her head against his arm.

His mother's smile fell into a tight purse, obviously catching on whatever thread his wife had thrown to her.

"What are you getting at, Princess?" grunted General Beakpoint, "What does his parentage have to do—"

"And she died last spring, from what Nilos told me," continued Azalea, cutting her off. Nilos swallowed a snort at the frustration on the General's face. "Which is when he went inexplicably mad and assassinated Emperor Rallios. Then he opened the Rift, but why? To what end? What was his motivation?"

Azalea whirled away from them, and Nilos followed her to the maps spread out on the stone war table. She slammed her palms flat, growling as her eyes glowed.

"What are you talking about, Your Highness?" scoffed the general. "Harvan is a madman. Nothing he does makes sense. You cannot try to comprehend his decisions."

"We are missing something are we not?" asked Nilos, but his wife did not answer as she rearranged the model troops on the table.

"Harvan is not masterminding the armies!" exclaimed Azalea. "He's providing intelligence on basic troop movements, but Vadros is giving the orders." She moved a spare figure over to the outline of the Heirlight mountains. "We have not been able to recover all of our dead, have we?"

Nilos' heart sank as Azalea shoved wooden troops from the allied armies to lump them with the Karden forces.

"Not all, especially when they attack at night," gasped Idris.

"They are converting our fallen troops into Karden," finished Nilos, as Azalea shifted more and more wooden figures into a terrifying formation.

"Mother, General, you have to pull out!" thundered Nilos, whirling towards the women in the mirror. "This is not an invasion. It is a massacre. They are moving our joined armies further apart on the battle fronts to create a clear path. You need to join with King Brexten and solidify the armies as one main force."

"They are clearing a route between you to Arcadius!" shouted Azalea, "General Beakpoint, you need to rush the forces to join with my father."

A trumpet blasted from the depths of the mirror.

"We have to go," groaned Idris. "As soon as this battle is over, we will return to this. Contact King Brexten and tell him what you are seeing. I love you." She flicked her eyes to Azalea. "Do not let him make any foolish decisions, Azalea."

Azalea dipped her chin as she squeezed his hand.

"I will not, Your Majesty. Fight well, General!" The mirror went blank.

"Dearest." The unexpected pet name quelled the fear in Nilos' heart as his wife tugged at his sleeve. "You said Harvan was driven mad trying to cast a spell. What spell?"

"We do not know." Nilos dragged his hand down his face. "Therein lies the problem. Nobody knows. He destroyed half of the hunting lodge he was staying in. When they found him, he was curled into a ball screaming about voices." He kissed her hair. "Come, beloved, we must contact your father."

"Wait." Azalea pulled from him to pace a circuit around the table. "I need to have the pieces arranged so my father can act swiftly and effectively. To do that, I *need* to understand what

Harvan was doing before he went mad."

Nilos was halfway to the mirror when she yipped as if she had been struck.

"How did his mother die?"

"His mother died in childbirth." Nilos turned back to her. "It was quite a scandal because she had never remarried after my uncle's death. Aunt Myra would not allow herself a lover after that." Her glowing gaze unlocked a place in his mind he had ignored for the sheer impossibility of it all. "Azalea, I could kiss your mind if it were possible. Harvan attempted a resurrection spell."

"I have not studied spells in depth, but they are impossible, are they not?" A victorious smirk pulled at her lips.

"Yes, because necromancy has been forbidden for nearly a thousand years!" Nilos grabbed his wife by the arms and kissed her fiercely. "He must have come across information on Vadros while researching resurrection spells, which is why he would have set out to break the Rift!" He released his brilliant bride and started again to the mirror to contact her father.

"Who attended the birth?" asked Azalea, her voice soft. "Dearest, who was his mother's midwife?"

Nilos froze in his tracks, and the sudden ice flooding his veins was colder than the dying blizzard beyond the window.

"My mother," he murmured, "She was down in the city when Aunt Myra went into early labor." The screams of grief that had echoed down the hall, accompanied by his mother's burning sun magic still haunted his dreams. "The baby was far too early, and, though my mother is an expert in healing magic, she could not stop the bleeding. Little Ivaline was born in the embrace of the gods, and Aunt Myra followed her daughter into their hall shortly after naming her." He rubbed his face, swallowing past the ache in his chest.

They both jumped as Lyric slammed through the door with a massive volume in his arms.

"Your Highnesses!" The boy slid to a stop. "I found it! I found the Rift spell."

"Show us," demanded Azalea.

Lyric shoved the book onto the table and opened to a marked page.

"To undo the sacrifice of fallen allies," read Nilos as Azalea joined him, "A dagger blessed by the priests of the sun must draw the blood of the whitest star. Under the shadow of the dark moon, pour it upon the highest peak of Light's Heir."

"Lyric, take this to Jarrett and have him contact the Archivists of Dawncliff," snapped Azalea, "Then relay it to the Arcadius Historians. They might yet find a way to reseal the Rift." The boy scurried from the room, but Nilos' heart ached at the senseless loss Harvan had first struck upon his family.

"Why my father?" he whispered, "Harvan and I were alone so many times the week my mother and aunt were tending his wounds." Nilos buried his face in his wife's hair. "He could have killed a dozen times over, so why did he choose my father? My blood is Whitestar, and, without a royal marriage, the alliance would likely never have been forged."

Azalea was no stranger to the guilt of a survivor of battle, and she wrapped her husband in her arms. He had yet to express his grief over his father in front of her, and she did not want to sully the memory of the man. The suspicion connected everything so clearly, with ice blue eyes and a thin-lipped stare.

"Dearest, please do not be angry with me, but I have to ask you a question." Those same eyes ached down at her, so much gentler than the ones trying to silence her from the wall. "What is the possibility that the Emperor was the father of the baby?"

Her husband jerked away from her, disbelief raging on his face.

"How could you even consider that?" Then, he froze, his hands falling limply to his side. "The Solstice feast…" Nilos' voice trailed off. He gripped the table and shook his head. "Mother had been in Arcadius overseeing the final tests of the Royal Academy, before they dismissed for the winter. An ice storm hit Arcadius and delayed her return."

Azalea rubbed his arm, as he squeezed his eyes and choked out a gasp.

"The storm missed Sardit, and we carried on the festival as usual." The maps crinkled under his grip. "I was not sober for most of it. Hardly any of us were. As you have seen, there is not much to do during the winter. But, Father, I remember him dancing with Aunt Myra. I think—I think too much to be proper—but I was occupied with a water mage with lips like—" he cut himself off, and Azalea snorted when his cheeks flushed. Her husband gifted her with a sorrowful smile. "The water mage's husband was quite thrilled of the possibility, but I do not enjoy the company of both as you do, my love. Either way, when I returned to the dancing, my father and Aunt Myra were gone."

"Your face says it all, my grieving storm." Azalea kissed the edge of her husband's jaw. "Harvan wants revenge. He must have known the truth, and he chose your father because he blamed him." Her love's expression crumbled further, and his shoulders drooped under her touch. "Now, he will not rest until—"

Azalea was cut off when Nilos screamed without warning and propelled away from the table.

"No! No!"

"What is wrong?" Heart racing, she reached for him, only for Nilos to stumble back and sink to his knees. He covered his head, his sobs booming out in deafening cracks.

The storm in Nilos' veins raged at the pain tearing his heart. It shattered, spilling from his body before he could stop it. He knew the feeling and what it meant, but he refused to accept it breaking his soul for the second time in months. Lightning cracked from his fingers and shattered a window. Wind swirled around the room, scattering the maps and papers in a tempest.

"No!" He roared to the gods, and he barely registered Jarrett and Robin bursting in. "Mother! No!"

"Get out!" Azalea's scream barely reached him, and he refused to accept the truth burning across the leagues of land between him and the battlefield. "Leave us! I will tend to him!"

His maelstrom whipped around him, and he had no desire to stop it as he rocked in its gale.

"Nilos!" calloused hands tugged at his arms, but he could not look up nor see past the dying light on the horizon. "What is wrong?" Warm arms embraced him, and petal soft lips broke past his storm to caress his cheek. "Come back to me, my love."

Long Live The Empress

M*y love.*

The words brushed the storm aside, spreading like balm over the tear in his core. Nilos blinked past the torrents of his eyes to find Azalea kneeling before him, tears staining her bloody cheeks. Scratches etched her face, twinkling with shards of glass. Every part of her was tense, shuddering, and Nilos cried out as he ripped his lightning from her skin back into his agonized soul.

"My love," whimpered Azalea. She pushed his arms way from his head. Her warm weight filled his lap, and he clung to her as her lips pressed into his face. "What has happened to you? Tell me. Tell your wolf what pains you so deeply."

"You are hurt." Nilos raised a trembling finger to a dark spot on her brow and winced as he pulled the nub of a quill from her skin. His pain broiled again, seizing his magic and ripping it. Another curse at the gods tore from him in a boom of thunder. First his mother, and now he had harmed his wife, his heart.

"Nilos, please, speak to me, my love." Her lips pressed into his, and the storm recoiled to swirl around the fading light that linked it to the first breath of life. The light blazed, then vanished, and the pain renewed the aching loss he had worked so hard to heal.

"She is dead," croaked Nilos. He buried his face in his wife's bosom, clinging to her with all he had to keep his storm from laying waste to the lands.

"Who has died, my love?" Azalea's hands were soft on his back, and she kissed his head over and over.

"My mother." At the confession, the hurricane in his soul spun with renewed anguish. "I felt it."

"Are you sure?" Her question did not come with doubt, and Nilos breathed in her sweet scent to center himself.

"Children are bonded to their parents' magic." His heart ached at the words. The wound left by his father widened to engulf the place his mother had held. "I felt her as surely as I felt my father."

"Oh, my gentle storm," sobbed his wolf, and her tears were wet upon his scalp as she cradled him.

Azalea did not count the time she spent holding her husband together. She simply let him sob into her embrace while the winds and static of his magic laid further waste to the room. The glass doors and windows had shattered under the tempest of his first outburst, and the whirlwinds had impaled broken quills and slivered shards of glass into her face and arms.

It was not until she had begun to shiver from the last vestiges of the storm outside pouring in that her Prince lifted his head to stare blankly at her. His normally warm and inviting gaze was as empty and frigid as the daggers of ice that hung from the outcropping of their bedroom window.

"I did not mean to hurt you," said Nilos, but there was no emotion in his words. Like before, he plucked something from her skin and let out a ragged noise.

"Just some scrapes." Azalea lied. Her skin burned and pinched from the dozens of injuries still piercing it. She could not let him break again. He had to get up. He had to put aside his grief and be strong for a few more hours. "I have had worse." She consoled him. "They will heal."

A soft knock echoed from the door.

"Enter," called Azalea, "but be careful. There is glass on the floor."

The door opened to reveal Sylva, Deidre, Asha-anne, and Jarrett clothed in black. The former nursemaid was the first to speak.

"We just received word from the battlefront."

Nilos nodded, and Azalea crawled out of his lap to help him to his feet.

"I know," stated her husband, his face still a mask of ice. "Please tend to my wife's wounds. I must go and pray."

Azalea did not want to leave him, but every Zelarian present fixed her with a look that told her not to intervene. She did not protest as Sylva wrapped an arm around her shoulder and pulled her into the hall.

Deidre let out a wail, hands bursting into flames, but Jarrett wrapped her in her arms before Azalea could get to her. Then, to her surprise, the knight scooped the weeping woman into his arms like a babe and carried her away. The skin on his neck flushed red, bubbling under her scalding touch. Asha-anne followed after them, leaving Azalea to be escorted by the very woman who was the primary thorn in Azalea's side.

The corridors were dark, as servants quenched the torches and replaced them with glowing orbs veiled in gauzy material. Nobody spoke, though they wept openly and curtsied to her when Azalea and Sylva passed.

From somewhere in the city, a bell tolled mournfully. The rolling gong echoed through the windows, breaking something loose inside of Azalea, and her soul-wolf crouched to keen and whimper at its sound. She had hardly known the Empress, but the devotion displayed by servants and family alike amplified the grief she carried on her husband's behalf.

"I am sorry for your loss," whispered Azalea to the older woman leading her to the room she had come to loathe. As the door opened, the pastel paintings and spring motifs were forlorn instead of overbearingly sweet.

"You know better than I the hazards of war, Princess." Sylva sniffled. She waved Azalea to a chair beside the fire instead of the narrow lounging couch where she normally examined her. "But I am grateful for your sympathies."

Azalea had no response for the woman's gentle tone nor the tears on her typically stern face. So, she sat silently and allowed Lady Sylva remove the debris from her skin and rinse the wounds with herbal astringents. She did not permit a hiss or complaint from the stings escape, because they were minuscule in the open pain before her.

The pine and nature scent of the woman's magic was not as cloying as Azalea had come to feel it, when Sylva ran her glowing hand over her skin. Mingled with the scent of the woman's tears, she was reminded of her damp pillow the night before she left the sea.

The gong of the bell rang through the palace again.

"If I have a daughter," murmured Azalea, "I shall name her Idris."

Sylva's glowing hand froze, and the woman finally cried aloud.

Like she had done for dozens of families upon return from battle, Azalea let her aunt weep into her shoulder and assured her softly that the gods had welcomed her sister home with all the honors of befitting a heroine.

On the other side of the castle, Nilos sat silently in his parents' empty bed chambers. He ran his fingers along the bottles of flower oils his mother had worn in her hair and on her skin. He did not hold back his tears when he moved over to the heavy cerulean cloak that had been worn by his father the last time Nilos had seen him hold court.

His mother had left it where it had lain, draped over the back of his father's favorite reading chair. He ran his palm along the fur at the collar and heaved a sigh. The solid strength of his father's magic had long since faded from its softness.

Nilos continued around the room until he found himself at the transparent silver curtains that covered his mother's private shrine to the gods. He pulled back the thin silk and snapped a bolt of lightning to the charred wick of the oil lantern suspended above it. The porcelain bowl his mother used for personal offerings caught his eye when it reflected back the small flame.

Nilos sank to his knees, choking out a sob at its contents. A single lock of his infant hair was wrapped around the shriveled, wilted petals of an azalea blossom.

"Even knowing you would face battle, your last prayer in this room was for my happiness." He touched the gold and silver threads that bound the prayer together and then touched his lips. The soft warmth of her magic was barely tangible. "A ruler is selfless, compassionate, fair, and kind." He recited the mantra she had instilled in him since childhood. "You embodied that more than I ever could."

Golden light swirled around the shrine and settled onto the wilted petal in the bowl.

"Mother," whispered Nilos. He reached for the sparkling

essence. "Please do not go." The azalea blossom glowed, and the wilted brown and blackened pigment turned radiant white and royal violet. The glittering light circled around his wrist thrice before dissipating into a cloud of sparks. He lowered his hand to the prayer bowl and grazed his fingers across the petal. Her final message gave him the strength to wipe his burning face and will his storm into submission.

"She called me her love," he whispered to the empty room. "That is all you wanted, for us to find love with each other."

The bell of the city cathedral tolled in its cloister again, as it had before. He lifted his face to the stars and sent his mother the softest of breezes to carry her spirit into the halls of the gods.

Lowering his head, he pressed his knuckles to his lips and waited, breathless. The final, largest bell echoed into the room, and he counted as the rest joined in.

Twelve times they rang out. Twelve times his heart broke in succession.

Then, from the outside of the castle walls, the songs of mourning lifted up from the citizens and carried in muffled tones over the grounds. He stood and trudged through the bogs of his grief to stare out over the snow.

The blizzard had turned to the smallest of flurries, and twilight was settling over the land. The solar mage of Zelarum had spent her last sunset to give him the fortitude to face what lay before him.

Beyond the walls, the yellow glows of candles flickered to life in the dark windows of every home. Then, slowly they moved to the street. Every citizen, whether man, woman, or child, was making their way to the castle gates. Their procession would soon fill the snow-covered palace grounds.

Nilos turned from the sight and stepped into the hall. Asha-anne was waiting, a shining black cloak in one hand and his platinum and sapphire coronet in the other.

He took the cloak from her and pulled it around his shoulders, fastening the silver clasp at his throat, and he bowed to let her slide the heavy weight onto his brow. Then he hugged his nursemaid, kissing the tears from her cheek.

Nilos curled his arm around her shaking shoulders as they walked to the top of the staircase. Azalea waited for him, her face free of the injuries he had inadvertently caused, wearing the black mourning robes of his people. Her hair had been combed from its usual braid so it fell in golden waves to her waist. The crown she had been born to bear adorned her brow in pearls and diamonds. His golden wolf wept openly, clinging tightly to his aunt's hand, and Nilos had never loved anyone so deeply.

Azalea extended her arm to her husband, and, silently, they made their way down the stairs. She did not know what waited. Sylva had simply instructed her to follow Nilos' lead. She looked up at her husband, whose face was graver than death's own mask. Later, she knew, he would truly grieve. Now was the time for strength. That, she could give him. That, she knew how to do.

The black-robed mages at the castle entrance bowed low and pulled open the doors, and the wordless singing that had carried into the castle broke over her.

Citizens of all ages stood at the base of the stairs, candles and lanterns in hand, as tears sparkled like liquid gold on every face.

Azalea squeezed Nilos' arm when he froze, and his own tears spilled fresh onto his cheeks.

"I love you," she murmured, and his oceanic gaze found hers. Finally, the light that had been missing filled their depths. "I am with you, always and eternally."

Azalea's earnest words were all Nilos needed. The love glowed golden yellow from her eyes, filling him with the courage to face what he was about to accept.

"Always and eternally," he responded and stepped out to face his people.

The singing came to a whispering halt, at the sight of the Prince and Princess framed by the glow the palace.

Nilos raised his left hand skyward, and, with a cacophony, he let loose his grief and the grief of all of Zelarum into the heavens. The lightning bolt crackled from his body, never seeming to end, pulling at his energy but not tiring him. It struck pierced the snow clouds above, surging out to spread their pain through the frozen droplets in their depths. The snow reflected the purple-white anguish back, lighting the world around them like dawn breaking through the horizon. Then, he silenced it and lowered his hand to place it over his heart.

He gave his voice thunder to carry his words to the citizens below.

"Empress Idris has fallen in battle. The Empress has passed into the hall of the gods. The Empress is dead!"

Azalea and her soul-wolf marveled at the raw display of emotion and power from her husband. When it shrank back into him, something was changed. His once graceful and gentle posture tensed under a burden more than the losses he had endured. His voice was strong, but she had come to know the soft stain of fear and uncertainty he could not hide from her.

Silence fell, and his eyes never left the crowd of people lit by candles before them. He seemed to be waiting, almost as if for the executioner's axe to fall. She followed his gaze out to the citizens.

They were silent as they glanced towards each other. Whispers broke free, rustling in small bursts, until one by one, each person raised a hand towards Azalea and Nilos.

Magic flowed from their upturned palms—a rainbow of light, petals, vines, fire, water, wind, sand, snowflakes, and shadows. It did not travel upwards to join the lightning still crackling in the sky. Azalea gasped as it crashed over them, whipping his cloak and her dress, warming her skin, filling her with spring blooms and summer grass. The tangible kaleidoscope twisted and tangled, settling over their bodies, wrapping around their joined arms like gilded armor.

Azalea's heart sang, and the wolf stirred with an approving hum at the unmistakable feelings of love and trust that filled her from the people's magic.

She glanced at her husband, and her heart swelled when she found his coronet had been replaced by a larger crown. It was taller, broader, and imposing in its platinum spikes with diamond and sapphire adornments. She had only seen it in portraits covered in the black veil of mourning and hanging in the war room.

Her own crown warmed against her hair, growing heavier, and she swallowed as she understood. Her husband looked down, and his mother's diadem reflected back at her from his eyes.

As if someone had given a silent signal, the voice of the people came together as one, and the palace grounds echoed out the call. The words reverberated off of the mountains behind them, rolling back, until it was a roar that set her wolf to howling in her core.

"Long live the Emperor! Long live the Empress!"

The heaviness of reality mingled with the unfamiliar crown on her head, and Azalea understood what had weighted down her husband on their journey to the door. It was the hope and terror of his people. She gazed back over the crowd and corrected herself. It was the hope and terror of *their* people.

"Long live the Emperor," whispered Azalea, when her husband turned to take her waist.

"Long live the Empress," he answered before bending low to press his lips to hers.

He tasted of salt, and Azalea breathed strength into his lungs to soothe his pain as their people continued to chant.

Challenge in Fire

zalea had witnessed the fall of a leader spread dismay and disorder amongst armies before, but her respect for the people of Zelarum had multiplied when Idris' death became the rallying moment for the otherwise peaceful nation.

The morning after the Empress's death, she had found what felt like most of the city waiting on the palace grounds. They had cleared the snow to expand the training area for the guards, and every able-bodied person was armed with anything that could be used as a weapon. Nilos was likewise bombarded with messages from villages and towns of citizens reporting they were sending more volunteers to the larger cities to train.

Her father had sent more soldiers northward into Zelarum to supplement their standing forces in the cities and assist with the training, but the battle that cost Idris and nearly two hundred soldiers from the allied forces their lives had forced the armies back as Azalea had predicted. There were not enough battle mages to supplement the Tyldonian forces while also maintaining the magical barriers protecting the cities caught in the warpath.

Azalea wanted nothing more than to armor herself and ride south to join in, but she and Jarrett were the only individuals who had seen combat and could train the ever-growing number of volunteers. The Zelarian advisors were ever adamant about producing an heir. Nilos' cousins on his father's side were not yet of age, and, if the Emperor fell, the throne would be at the will of the counsel.

One week after the fall of the Empress, they received their first communication from Harvan, and the threat was not only towards the newly crowned Emperor.

The soldier King Brexten had sent to assist Azalea and Jarrett with training had arrived on a Zelarian steed, her heart missing and her eyes plucked from her skull. She was long since dead, but her blood was smeared in three words across the stallion's frothy coat.

Everyone will burn.

The emissary's pyre was still blazing when Azalea stared out the window of her chamber to the otherwise darkened grounds. Nilos heaved another log into the hearth behind her, and she could not take the silence that had stretched between them since the short funeral any longer.

"I want to take the battle to Harvan and Vadros." Azalea turned to her husband.

Nilos looked up from his high-backed chair, his blue eyes drawn and weary, but she did not give him space to speak.

"I do not care what the laws state," she insisted and crossed the room. "He will come for us regardless, and we will still face him in battle. I will not sit by and wait for him to trap us."

"You are right," admitted Nilos. Azalea paused, unprepared for his agreement. "I cannot sit idle while our people shed blood. I have never wanted to sit idle, but I knew my duties. Now, my duty is for the glory or the fall of an empire."

"When, then?" She crossed her arms. Her husband stood

and rubbed his face. "We will need at least two days to ready supplies for a journey in this weather."

"I am meeting with the Tyldonian Archivists and the Historians at Arcadius via mirror tomorrow." Nilos pulled her hands into his. "This afternoon, they said they were close to developing a spell to seal the Rift. Once I speak with them, you and I will begin preparations to join the armies."

"I will wait no longer than a week." Azalea went into his embrace, resting her cheek against his pounding heart. "With or without the spell, we ride to war."

"Tonight." His fingers were gentle against her loose hair as he toyed with a curl. "I wish to take my wife to bed and rectify the duties I have neglected these last two days as her lover." She lifted her face, welcoming his gentle lips when they teased along the curve of her nose. "If she is willing."

"She is willing," purred Azalea. Nothing else would serve to draw her thoughts from strategies and vengeance except his touch.

Nilos swept his lover into his arms, losing himself to the taste of her kiss. He carried her to their bed, easing her onto the blankets. He broke away only long enough for her to slide the heavy, single-layer gown she had taken to wearing in bed over her head. He shed his own shirt and loose trousers to join the pile of sage material on the rug.

"Lie back," he ordered softly, and he sent thanks to all the gods for the treasure before him as Azalea reclined against the pillow.

Groaning, he slipped between her parted thighs and teased the curve of her jaw with soft brushes of his lips. Azalea's fingers against his bare back were as tender, and he marveled at how his ferocious Empress could set aside her rage to be as soft and yielding as the petals of her namesake beneath him.

Shifting lower, he followed the fading evidence of their last impassioned coupling down the satin of her chest to the dusky pink bud peaking her right breast. He moaned as he captured it in his lips, savoring the breathy whimpers that escaped her. Slowly, he swirled his tongue, and Azalea arched into the fingers he slipped them down her hips until he found the golden crown between her thighs.

He released her breast with a gentle graze of his teeth and caught the left in a gentle bite in time to the first touch of her most sensitive places. She shivered under him, her fingers dragging down his spine.

Nilos slid down her body, nipping at the space just above her navel to earn himself another whimper of his name, until he was prostrate between her knees. With a groan, he pulled her to his tongue, tasting the first drops of her arousal that glistened from her center. Azalea's fingers laced with his on her stomach.

His sweet wolf keened above him as he slipped his tongue into her warmth, drawing more of her tart nectar into his mouth. Nilos laved the sticky wetness up, seeking his prize, and swirled his tongue against the pliant nub at the apex of her pleasure.

"Softer," she gasped, her fingers raking across his scalp. He paused, glancing up. Her glowing gaze met his, shimmering with her need. "I am more sensitive than usual this evening."

Holding her eyes, Nilos eased his tongue forward for a softer, teasing stroke. Azalea's head fell back, and she mewled his name.

Closing his eyes, he freed a hand from her grip to ease, first one, and, then a second, finger into her soaking heat.

If his wife needed him gently, he would satisfy her every demand.

Already, she was fluttering around him. Her fingers tightened in his as her other ran across his hair. He sucked gently, matching the slow, deep, languorous thrusts of his hand. Mere seconds of touch, and he had Azalea teetering on the cusp of release.

She clenched around him, lifting from the blankets as she sobbed out her pleasure. Nilos released her from his lips gingerly, his own arousal flexing where it was pinned between his stomach and the blankets, as he drew his wife down from the stars with teasing licks of the pleasure swollen bud.

"Kiss me," pleaded Azalea. Stars danced across her vision, and the ocean crashed in her ears.

Nilos was over her swiftly, his lips soft but urgent as he rocked his hardened body against her. She caught his lower lip between hers, cleaning her own, wet completion from his skin. Azalea reached between them, taking him in hand, and guided him into herself with a single motion.

"Stars, beloved," groaned her storm, as he filled her slowly. "You are always so wet and warm for me. Each time, I feel as if I have fallen into the spring of the gods."

"When you fill me," she murmured against his cheek, her body singing in the glorious perfection of his slow, stretching, strokes. "I feel your soul against mine. I do not want to be parted from you."

"We will never be parted." Nilos's promise pulled her back to his kiss, and Azalea wrapped herself around her husband. His arms folded under her, encasing her in a sanctuary of love and soft blankets, and the world around her was blocked out by the bliss of his weight.

Her skin tingled, as if his magic washed across her, but he had not released a single spark onto her body. The wolf was subdued, drowning in the pleasure her storm breezed across her.

With each stroke, kiss, and pant of her name, the aftershocks of her first release grew tighter. Azalea whined into her lover's parted lips, pawing at his back as she tried to hold back the impending flight into the clouds. She wanted to finish with him.

"Fall with me." Nilos squeezed her tighter to him, never faltering.

"I love you," gasped Azalea, and she silenced her howl with his tongue. His chest deep groan filled her mind, mingling with the ringing and humming that sang from the stars bursting to life under her skin.

Nilos thrust twice more, then held himself deep within her. The short, reflexive ruts of his release rocked him against her, amplifying her tumble into their joined releases.

"You weep." Her husband's thumb was soft as he stroked her cheek. "Why? Did I hurt you?"

"Because I have never felt more at peace than I do when you love me so softly." The confession caught Azalea by surprise, and a tear sparkled from the corner of his right eye. "The thought of losing—" Her husband kissed her again and slipped from inside of her. Azalea ached at the absence, and she clung to him when he rolled onto his side and pulled her into his chest.

"Sitting there, watching you at the window." Nilos' gaze burned into hers, and Azalea found it difficult to breathe from the intensity sparking behind them. "I realized that if anyone tried to take you from me, I would tear the world from its foundations and cast the sky from its zenith to bring you back into my arms." The lethal finality to his words contrasted the careful caress of his fingers against her back. "What should terrify me, but does not, is that I would feel no guilt as I watched the stars rain from the sky so long as it brought us back together."

"I pity any who think to keep the Golden Wolf from her Stormwielder." Azalea caught his lip with her thumb and hummed when he bit the soft skin gently. "On our wedding day, I was certain we would never find more than cordial agreeance, but each day you sink deeper and deeper into my soul."

"I first knew I would love you when you cried over your brother at the wedding." Nilos kissed the meaty portion of her palm. "I doubted that you would ever love me, and I have never been more pleased with being proven wrong." His wife's flushed cheeks darkened, and her furrowed brow softened.

"When this war is over." Her words were hesitant, and Nilos treated himself to another taste of her skin at the curve of her wrist. "When we return, I will not reside in my personal chambers." He paused, enjoying the sensation of her pulse against his lips. "I want to sleep each night and wake each morning in your arms."

Nilos grinned and kissed the racing beat of her heart twice before pulling her arm around his waist.

"Before we leave, I will ask the staff to move our things into my parents' former chambers." He kissed her brow, adoring the soft sighs and the way Azalea attempted to wriggle even closer to him. "I will have your chambers converted to a room for your parents. The nursery and nursemaid suite beside it can be remade into a room for Rex and his nanny when they visit."

"Thank you." Azalea's hand brushed lazily against his spine, and her eyes fell half shut below him as he kneaded her bare rear.

Soon, he would have to pull the blankets over her to keep the chill from her skin, but Nilos would not move until she needed it.

Their peace was short lived, because someone pounded against the door.

"Nilos!" shouted Jarrett from the other side. "Azalea. Quickly. You are needed!"

"No titles," grunted his wife, as she rolled away from him. "This must be urgent."

"Let us dress!" shouted Nilos.

"Do not bother with finery!" came the knight's sharp reply.

Azalea tossed him his clothes before yanking her thick gown over her body and tying her heavy dressing robe.

She eased the fleece lined slippers onto her feet, ripped the door open, and stumbled to a stop at the pair before her.

Jarrett's normally neat hair was unkempt and possibly singed, and small, finger-like welts were scattered over his bare chest. Mouth shaped scald marks spotted his strong neck.

"If you are interrupting us because you made the mistake of fighting Deidre," snorted Nilos.

"Fighting is not the word I would use," giggled Azalea, "Although I would see about a balm for that love bite just under your ear there. It may blister."

"Follow me." Jarrett sprinted down the hall, and Azalea took off after him. She had never known him, even in crisis, to resist a joke about his intimate exploits.

Nilos followed wordlessly after his wife's knight, uncertain what was coming when the man shoved through the door to the observatory tower. He kept his hand against Azalea's back, balancing her with his magic as she hitched her skirts and jogged up the stairs.

Deidre was waiting near a pile of cushions and blankets. An empty wine bottle lay discarded near a tray of cakes and fruit, and his cousin tugged a blanket around the over-sized shirt she had obviously thrown on in her haste. He arched a brow at her, smirking. She made a rude gesture, and her cheeks flushed.

"Lecture me later," snapped Deidre, "Look!" He followed her finger towards the southernmost window, where Jarrett had dragged the telescope for them to apparently stargaze from inside.

"What is that?" asked Azalea, shifting towards it.

"A telescope," he replied, earning him a sharp smack on the arm from his wife.

"I know what a telescope is. I meant *that!*" She pointed again, her eyes narrowed and feral yellow with the power of her wolf. "What does that say? It is words."

Nilos rushed forward and bent to squint into the viewer. The sky to the south, to the east of Arcadius, was ablaze.

"Azalea," he snarled, "See for yourself."

The storm raged in his core, and he squeezed her shoulders to keep himself from losing control.

Azalea bent low, and the wolf in her soul grew wild in its fury.

There, burning against the clouds, were the words that solidified her hunger for Harvan and Vadros' deaths.

Arcadius will fall first.

It was a challenge, and one she would meet with gladness.

"We ride out at noon," she growled, shoving the telescope away. "Jarrett, wake Asha-anne and Sylva. Have Captain Shara prepare the guard. Leave only who is necessary to fortify the walls."

"Deidre, go to the kitchens and have the night cooks begin packing at least two days' worth of rations for the guard," ordered Nilos, "You will hold the throne in our absence, cousin. I will leave word—"

"Not on your life," scoffed the woman, and Azalea smirked when she crossed her arms. "I did not spend the last two months training just to sit here and play steward. Where the three of you go, I go."

"I would not have it any other way." Azalea hugged the woman. "Vadros has no idea what he is about to face if you get your fire on him."

"Fine." Nilos knew it was pointless to argue, so he threw up his hands at the stubborn women before him. "Once you have put out the orders, wake your mother and inform her of what is coming. Then, you are both to go to bed and rest." He jabbed a finger at the knight and his cousin. "I mean it, rest. We will be riding hard and fast."

"I will summon the counsel," said Azalea, already at the door to the stairs.

"First, we must contact your father." Nilos took her arm, hurrying her down the stairs.

The palace was slowly waking, as the guards on the southern walls had obviously caught sight of what hung in the sky. He paid them no mind as he raced hand in hand with his wolf to the war room.

No sooner had the door closed than Nilos hit the frame of the enchanted mirror with his magic. It shimmered to life, and a Tyldonian guard came into view.

"Princess, I mean Empress Azalea." The woman snapped to

attention. The tent flap behind her flew open.

"I need to speak with my daughter," came King Brexten's rough growl. "Activate the mirror—oh, Azalea!" A fresh scar ran down his face from brow to jaw.

"Papa!" Nilos released his wife's hand as she reached up to touch the frame. It was the first time she had spoken with him directly since the war. Each time they had contacted the front, he had been at the head of the forces.

"Sweet pup." The king's face lost its sharpness. "How I have missed you."

"I will be joining you soon." Nilos rubbed Azalea's back when she pulled her hand away from the mirror. "We just saw the challenge. We are riding at noon for Arcadius."

"But the laws of Zelarum—" began the king, and Nilos cut him off.

"We make the laws, Brexten, and we have decided the law is outdated and useless." Nilos curled his arm around his wife as she stepped into his side. "Azalea and I will meet our enemies in battle." Glancing down, he found his golden wolf grinning wildly up at him. Already, the lust for battle glowed in her eyes. "We will emerge victorious, or we will pass into the halls of the gods." She stroked his jaw, and Nilos kissed her palm. "Whatever the outcome, we go together, always together."

"A wolf does not cower when her pack is in danger." Azalea drew herself up, turning towards her father. The surprise she found waiting on his battle-weary face was equal parts hope and horror. "Neither does an Empress." She held her father's gaze, and she filled her voice with the authority granted her by the Star Makers and the Sun Raisers. "The Wolf Empress of Zelarum will not sit idle while all she loves is laid to waste. She will unleash her fury upon any who threaten what is sacred."

"And the Storm Emperor will carry her rage on his thunder." Nilos' skin sparked under her palm, and she did not need to look up to know his eyes were flashing with his power.

"Love suits you far fairer than any crown, my ferocious daughter." King Brexten's smile was forced, but the affection was obvious in his hazel eyes. "We will be at Arcadius by midmorning. I have already began marching the best of my troops."

"I will listen for your roar." Azalea softened in his arms, and Nilos held her all the more tighter. "May the sun be ever at your back, Papa."

"And may the stars guide your journey." The Zelarian blessing in her father's rough voice spoke all Azalea needed to hear. He saw her love, and he accepted its truth. The mirror shimmered until only their reflections remained.

"We will stop them," swore her husband, and Azalea turned in his arms to hold him. "We will not let either land fall to ruin."

"We should alert the counsel now," she murmured.

It was nearing midnight when they dismissed the counsel and stole back to the solace of their room. In the warmth of their blankets and the dark of the night, Nilos held his goddess in his arms. Her lips moved in soundless words against his chest, and he joined her in her silent prayers to beg the gods to never allow them to be separated by death.

The Pain of Victory

After a day and night of riding through biting winds, Nilos welcome the morning sun as it rose over the forest. Its light warmed the protective plates over his vital organs and the leather armor on his limbs. Azalea, he knew, would have preferred he be covered from head to toe in the enchanted metal, but he needed to be free to move and direct the storm when they reached Arcadius.

The call to arms had been greater than he expected, and he glanced back again at the nearly three hundred citizens who had come to fight alongside their Emperor and Empress. As they traveled through the forest, another hundred had joined from the farming villages that spanned the frozen but fertile fields throughout the woods. Nilos had never led a force larger than fifty, but his wife had given him no time to flounder for the unanticipated numbers.

Azalea had taken command with charismatic confidence that bolstered even the most hesitant of the volunteers. Seeing the same people who likely scorned the wedding look to her with hope and faith filled Nilos with assurance that victory was theirs to take. Watching her standing high upon a supply wagon—eyes aglow—was a sight he would remember until his dying breath.

He had seen her in scuffed training armor, the finest gowns, and only firelight and moonbeams. Those were nothing compared to the first rays of dawn sparkling off of the armor he had no idea his mother had commissioned for her as a wedding gift. The golden, fur-like etching was spotted with enchanted crystals to supplement its protection, and the wolf-shaped helm beneath her arm held two massive sapphires filled with healing magic that would activate if she bled more than a surface wound.

"Once we break from the tree line," called Azalea, "We will be exposed between here and Arcadius. Stay close, shield bearers on the outer ranks. Those with weapons stay paired with someone whose magic is more defensive." She scanned the myriad of armored guards and terrified farmers, praying they could not see the fear churning in her core.

If she had had cavalry, pike-men, swordsmen, and archers, she would already have pushed them out of the forest. Commanding half a legion of mages with no experience in small conflicts, much less a full-scale battle, was never something she'd prepared for. Understanding the subtleties of how each personality impacted the force and methods of their power was too intricate for the scant months she'd spent amongst them.

Azalea glanced to her husband, who was still mounted on Anurob. Nilos' adoring expression and his broad smile assured her she was handling the assignment of positions and duties well.

"Royal guard, you know your duties," she finished and met Captain Shara's gaze. The older woman nodded to her and then Jarrett. "The edge of the forest is about an hour ride for those of us at the front. Healers, make sure you a riding the outer ranks to pass it along to the forces in the back. Do not let the wait as we pull free of the treeline steal your courage."

She dropped to the forest floor and seized hold of her mare from Deidre.

"You stay close to Jarrett," she whispered, "If I am severely wounded, he may lose himself to a blood fury. Do not let him surrender his position to reach me."

"I will do my best," said Deidre, and Azalea hauled herself into her saddle. The lighter, Zelarian armor was a change from the usual weight she bore, but she did not doubt that the armor smiths had put their best work into its creation.

"At your word, Empress," said Nilos, and Azalea pulled her helm over the tight, knotted braid that Sylva had woven at the base of her neck.

"Onward!" she cried and nudged her mare into motion.

Nilos did not speak, and Azalea was grateful. Her soul-wolf was on alert, catching each change in the breeze and each sound of the forest.

The sun had barely touched the lower branches when the south wind flooded her face with traces of smoke, blood, death, and the stench of the Karden.

Yipping, Azalea spurred her mount into a canter, chasing the familiar fragrance of battle and victory. The sound of metal, screaming, and the orchestra of Tyldonian animalistic war cries reached her in a messy roar. She broke through the tree line first, and she howled her arrival across the siege taking place in the city at the base of the gently sloping, snow-covered hill. The armies below were a tangle in the reddish gray slush that filled the open fields.

The high wall of the city was alive with the prism of mage spells raining down on the forces below and securing the shimmering bubble encasing the top of the city. Tiny specks sped up the wall, only to be blasted away in a white-blue blaze as an arrow or spell found their mark.

When the petrichor of a storm mingled with ozone and thunder rolled past her, She howled again, kicking her mare into a gallop and drew her sword.

From the cacophony of battle came a familiar roar, and Azalea ripped her sword from its sheath. Her father was alive, and the Lion of Tyldon called for his Golden Wolf. She gave into the wolf, surrendering to the familiar, ravenous hunger for the hunt and the sweet satisfaction of glory.

Nilos released Anurob's reins, and the stallion charged after Azalea. The storm demanded release, and he cried out as he hurled a ball of lightning over the armies to hit a gaggle of Karden scurrying up the wall in the distance. He had only a moment to scan the armies, as they grew closer, but hope re-surged in force at the sight of mage and warrior melding blade and magic in a dance of chaos against the enemy.

Azalea hurled herself from her horse, plunging her sword into the back of a Karden and blocking the light beam of another with her shield. Nilos followed suit, hauling the mage she had saved to his feet and diving into the throes of battle after his Empress.

He struck out with his wind, snapping the heads clean of Karden bodies and piercing their eyes with bolts of lightning. Something struck the plates of his back, and when he whirled he found Jarrett ripping his sword from the back of a Karden skull.

The tiger bellowed his power, and a blast of fire consumed the body from Deidre's well-placed spell. Nilos cleared their way, following his wife's relentless slaughter, until a lion's roar rattled his bones.

Father and daughter were side by side, swords dripping, faces snarling in the absence of both of their helms, and Nilos released his rage in a curtain of lightning on the four Karden slashing at them. He looked around swiftly for Azalea's helm, terrified of her facing the enemy without the healing spells set within.

"We must protect the gates!" cried Brexten, "They have all but shattered them!"

"A whirlwind!" ordered Azalea, "Barricade it with your winds!"

Nilos called his storm around him and hurtled himself over the Tyldonian forces to the ramparts above. The mages cheered his arrival, and he sprinted to the arch that signified the rarely closed gates of Arcadius.

Azalea's heart swelled as the wolf howled praise to her mate. Lightning and wind rained down from above, striking below. He was safe, out of their reach, surrounded by the mages of the city that joined their Emperor.

She lost herself to the familiar dance of battle. With her father at her side and her husband above, she was not dismayed by the waves of Karden pushing them nearer and nearer the shattered gates.

"A group has broken over the west wall!" bellowed Jarrett, "They are heading into the city."

"Stop them," grunted her father, as he rammed his fists into the chest of a Karden. The creature's mottled heart seeped gray sludge from its cage in his armored fingers. "Go, now Azalea!"

"You five, with me!" she snarled at the soldiers and mages closest to her. Without looking back, she sprinted through the gap in her husband's onslaught of power and dashed inside the half-destroyed gate.

The street beyond was littered with burned bodies of soldiers, mages, and Karden alike. She leaped over them, glancing back only long enough to see her people were with her. Alleys and side streets had been barricaded by magic and overturned carts. Groups of mages stood in some, building walls of the earth and vines.

Shouts rang out from the southwest, and she whipped around abandoned market stalls to find herself in the circular city center. The temple of the Star Makers towered over her, and the fountain of their Queen, Estella, no longer poured water into its basin.

A sickly, cloying smell slammed into her, and pain tore at her joints. A blinding, white light enveloped her, seizing her muscles, and Azalea cried out when her sword and shield clattered from her hands. The she-wolf in her soul raged against the pain, lashing out, demanding to regain control of her body, but Azalea could barely breathe.

Her churning stomach dropped as she was jolted into the air. She whirled to the left, and power spiked through her, seizing her limbs as her heartbeat faltered and skipped. Welts burned across her skin as invisible tendrils ripped her gauntlets and gloves from her body. Her chest plate smashed into her head as it was torn away. Stars danced across her vision, and copper flooded her throat. She spun in the air, rising higher, until she found herself face to face with eyes as icy blue as her husband's but lacking all warmth. Their owner sneered as she struggled against his magic.

"Well what do I have here?" snickered Harvan. "A rabid wolf without her pack." She barely heard him over the ringing in her ears as the lightning released her. He thrust his hand to the side, and Azalea refused to scream when she was hurled through the stained-glass window behind him.

She whined when she hit the wall at the far end of the dusty attic of the cathedral. Her head spun as she staggered to her feet, pulling a dagger from her boot as she went. Her skin and muscles still burned with the unmistakable pain of her husband's magic.

Harvan stood before her, his blue eyes dancing madly. His smile was feral and yellowed.

"So this is the little princess my pathetic aunt forced onto my cousin." The pallid glow of his magic slicked around him in waves of decay. "I had heard you were a mighty warrior. Yet, you can barely stand."

Azalea fell forward to escape the wave of magic he hurled towards her. It caught her in her tumble, and the strength in her muscles drained under its grip.

"What is it they call you," taunted Harvan, "The Golden Wolf of Tyldon?" His boot collided with her head, and she snarled while the world turned over, engulfed in gray snow and black stars. "More like a quivering bitch." He circled her, cackling. Spittle dripped down his chin.

The wolf growled in her soul and reverberated through Azalea's chest as it regained its bearings. She struggled against the pain, standing squarely, forcing her trembling legs to hold her up. She dug another dagger from its hidden sheath against her hip. So many retorts danced on her tongue, but she chose the one she knew would make him most reckless. If she had learned one lesson of the mages, their magic was uncontrollable if they were driven to breaking.

"Says the man who could not pop his mother's breast from his mouth even as an adult." She smirked. "Were you jealous that your father's brother put a baby in her womb when you wanted it to be your seed growing there?"

"How dare you speak of her!" Harvan's magic flashed sickly green around him. "I will end you and everything you love, you whore!" The maddened mage lunged for her.

Azalea snarled in victory as he fell into her trap. She ducked, ramming the thick leather of her shoulder pad into his gut, and threw him over her back. She swirled on one foot and stomped on his spine.

Thunder cracked from below, and she growled at the nearness of her husband to the danger at her feet. She would end the pathetic life before her before he could even breathe the same air as her beloved.

Harvan rolled as she lifted her boot to stomp again, but when he flailed for her leg, Azalea kicked him in the jaw with a growl.

"I will take immense pleasure turning your intestines to leather for my armor," she snarled. Azalea raised her blade, but a blast of energy-sucking magic threw her backward.

She rolled over her shoulder as she landed, coming up in a crouch, holding her dagger at the ready. The wolf was all she knew, and the world tinted free of much of its color. All she could smell was the fear, the anger, and it burst into her nostrils with the pounding of the pulse in the exposed throat of her enemy.

Another blast of magic burst from Harvan. Azalea yowled as she was slammed into the wall near the shattered window.

"I will feast on your heart, Tyldonian cunt." Harvan prowled towards her, her first dagger shining in his grip. Azalea could not move under the weight of decay leeching at her arms and her chest. "The line of the Whitestars ends tonight. First with you, and then with that pretentious cousin of mine."

The dagger bit across her cheek, and Azalea howled in fury. Blood spilled across her lips as Harvan pulled the blade down to her barely exposed throat. An earth-shattering boom echoed around them, and her wolf-sensitive hearing burned and burst under the pressure.

Harvan stumbled back, covering his ears and screaming. His broken focus gave Azalea her body, and she staggered away from the wall. Her weak muscles pleaded with her to stop, to conserve her energy until reinforcements arrived, but she ignored them.

She jumped onto him, howling out her victory, though all she heard was white hot silence, as she swung the dagger down. The sharp blade sunk into Harvan's chest at the moment his fist collided with the soft spot beneath her ribs. Pain ripped through her, driving the air from her lungs. The dagger he had stolen found its way through the leather padding she'd worn beneath her armor. Victory gave way to mind numbing fear as she fell to the wood beside him.

He yanked free the dagger she had left in him, and it clattered to the floor. Azalea knew not to touch the one protruding from her own side, though it ripped and tore with each pant she sucked in. Blood pooled from Harvan's lips, bubbling as he coughed and twitched.

She winced when his freezing hand found hers between them, and fear stole all the madness from his glacial stare.

"Will it stop?" he gurgled, his hand limp against hers when she yanked it away. "Will the baby stop screaming in my thoughts?"

"You," grunted Azalea. The final piece fell into place. "You caused the early labor?"

"Will I see them again?"

"No," hissed Azalea. The burning in her side grew dreadfully colder. "You will never see your family again."

Harvan choked out a sob, and his chest rose no more. His eyes, so alike and so different to Nilos' dimmed, taking the light pouring into the attic with them.

"Nilos," gasped Azalea, and darkness yanked her from her mind without mercy.

Nilos had whirled around when Azalea's first howl of pain reached him from within the city.

"No!" he thundered, leaping from the wall to the roof of a nearby building. The distorted white light of Harvan's magic lit up the city center near the temple, and Nilos barreled across the roof when a golden figure flew into the air.

A different figure shadowed the highest balcony of the cathedral, his arms outstretched, and Nilos hurled a lighting bolt towards Harvan. His cousin moved, and the hovering Azalea intercepted his strike. Her scream tore at his heart and she spasmed in mid-air.

"No! No!" Nilos dodged a Karden who leaped at him from a nearby building, landing with a grunt only to find Jarrett and Deidre racing towards him.

"Vadros is in the sanctuary," panted Jarrett, "He has no

barriers around the door except the dead priests he has risen. That's where Harvan took Azalea."

"Can you still feel her?" snapped Nilos while they charged through the city.

"Yes, and to say she is angry is an understatement," huffed the knight. "She can hold her own against Harvan."

Nilos wanted nothing more than to launch himself skyward after her, but, with Vadros so close, he trusted his wolf to bring Harvan's terror to an end. Deidre's fire joined his lightning blast, and the still mutating, staggering, and hissing corpses before the open sanctuary doors erupted in a red mist.

Hands crackling, Nilos blew through the sizzling gore and landed halfway up the aisle to the altar where he had first met the keeper of his heart.

A figure stood before it, and its mottled, skeletal fingers reached up to lower its hood.

"You are brave to face me with so little support, my young Emperor." The voice sucked the warmth from Nilos' body, bringing images of death and shades to his heart. The face revealed before him was born of horrors.

Vadros cheeks clung to his skull, and his lips were thin and crinkled with the same gray goo that spilled from wounded Kardens. His eyelids sank into empty sockets, and a singular blue, human eye took up the entirety of his brow.

"This ends now," snarled Nilos, though the shadows teasing around the demon's robes seemed to suck hope from the air.

"Your ancestors failed to destroy me," chuckled Vadros, "and you believe you can? Already I have beaten your army and taken the sanctuary of your gods."

He raised his hands, and the same whitish blue light of the Karden's death blasts glowed from his fingers and his lone eye.

"Your magic is nothing, Stormwielder."

Nilos hurled his lightning forward, catching Vadros' blast before it could strike him. They bounced apart, striking the walls, and thundering through the floor.

"You think that is power?" laughed Vadros, but Nilos met his attack again, channeling his magic into the air above into thunderheads. Shouting, he rained them down as he hurled the ones in his core like spears.

Something burned past his ear, and Nilos yanked back his wind so Jarrett's arrow—surrounded with Deidre's flames— could sink into the monster's stomach.

Vadros howled, ripping it from his robes, as the tiger and the fire mage flanked Nilos.

Flames licked along Deidre's skin and blazed like a goddess's halo from the crown of her head. The embers that sparked from her nostrils when she huffed at the exertion from her power were something he had not seen before. She was gloriously terrifying.

"Together," hissed his cousin, and Jarrett answered with a feral rumble. The orange glow and bared teeth told Nilos the tiger was too far lost in rage for words.

The knight drew his sword, and Nilos grasped Deidre's hand to fuse their powers into a vortex of wind, fire, and lightning. Jarrett barreled through it, roaring as he slammed his blade into Vadros' shoulder, dragging down to his hip. The spasming, burning monster screeched when his arm and three of his ribs peeled away to melt into the stones.

With Deidre at his side, Nilos surged forward, striking again and again as Jarrett plunged his blade into the necromancer's gut, his chest, and his neck.

"Move!" boomed Nilos, and he ripped the dagger Azalea had

given him the morning they left Sardit from its sheath.

"This is for every soul you have stolen." Pouring what was left of his energy into the blade, Nilos slammed it into the monster's bubbling eye.

Blue light lit up behind the fetid skin, glowing brighter and brighter, and Nilos ripped the dagger free.

"Get back!" he warned, shoving his friends away with a blast of wind, but the monster's skull exploded in a boom that sent Nilos soaring. He grunted as he hit a pew, and the walls around them fractured and trembled. The light was never ending, building—blinding everything—and the noise did not cease.

Nilos covered his ears while the sound shattered through the windows, ripping out, and leaving him sightless from the sunspots that consumed his vision.

He staggered to his feet when Jarrett screamed as if he was struck.

"Azalea!" The knight's words barely pierced the ceaseless ringing in Nilos' ears. "Azalea!" The man staggered through the still burning sludge that had been Vadros. "Nilos! Where are the stairs!"

"What?" shouted Nilos, not sure what he was asking as the world spun and nausea ripped through him.

"Through the eastern door!" groaned Deidre. Nilos hauled her to her feet as Jarrett slammed into the door, screaming Azalea's name. Dread flooded Nilos, because there was only one thing that would make the knight so terrified.

He sprinted after him, grabbing both Jarrett's and Deidre's hand when they reached the circular staircase. With what energy he had left, he summoned a whirlwind and blew them up the seven flights of open space until they burst into the attic.

All he saw was the blood.

It spilled like a reflecting pool around the limp bodies near the broken window. Harvan was dead, he knew, because there was no taste of his magic in the air. Azalea lay on her back beside him, their fingers a breath apart. Her face and hands were as pale as the reaper's cloak.

"No!" he cried, sliding through the blood to grab the hilt of the dagger protruding from her side.

"Do not take it out!" hollered Jarrett. "She is alive, but, if you remove that, you will kill her!"

Deidre rushed past them to the window.

"The Kardens are retreating!" she shouted, "I can fetch a healer!"

"There is no time." The shaking knight seized Nilos by the shoulders. "Can you heal her? She is fading fast. I can barely feel her wolf. You have to heal her!"

"I have no skill for wounds like this." Nilos choked on his words. "Deidre? Have you—"

"I can seal the vessels with fire, but I cannot mend her flesh," his cousin panted, "It should be enough to get her to a healer."

"Nilos, hold her still. Even unconscious her body will jerk." Jarrett's voice cracked. "You cannot let her move even a tremor, or I may damage her worse when I remove the blade."

Nilos summoned the final dredges of his storm to pin his motionless wolf in place.

"As soon as I remove the dagger, Deidre, you cauterize the vessels and arteries."

Deidre nodded and positioned her hands over Azalea's bleeding side.

"Now!" Jarrett yanked the blade straight out, and the smell of burning flesh filled the air when Deidre closed her hands over the wound.

The blood popped and snapped like oil in a pan. His cousin's face grew pale as her strength ebbed. Nilos pressed his brow to hers, allowing her to draw from his life force, not caring that his world grew faint. She tumbled back with a breathless gasp.

Nilos glanced down. The bleeding had stopped, but the wound still gaped. Deidre dug a handkerchief from somewhere in her dress and covered it.

"Her face," murmured Nilos, "It is still bleeding."

Jarrett grabbed the heavy material of Deidre's sleeve and ripped it from shoulder to wrist. With deft fingers he tied it around Azalea's head.

Beyond their bubble of pain and exhaustion, the city resounded with a cheer of victory. Over the voices echoed a roar.

The Lion King of Tyldon called for his daughter. Tears soaked Nilos cheeks as he cradled the limp wolf in his arms. Another roar carried up to them, but Azalea did not open her eyes.

Reunited in Peace

Azalea was cold. She could not remember a time she had ever felt so consumed by frigid darkness. A blanket was tucked around her. She could feel its weight and where it wrinkled under her back, but she was frozen deep in her bones. Everything was encased in ice, except her throat.

Her throat was on fire.

She could not move. Trying to open her eyelids was a labor of will that burdened her down, but she needed to quench the inferno in her throat. She could not swallow. Her lips stuck together and tore painfully when she cracked them open.

"Shh." A grandfatherly voice came from somewhere to her left. She tried to turn her head, but horses stampeded in her skull. "There, there, Your Majesty." Soft, weathered hands cupped the back of her head, and the cool wood of a cup pressed against her lips.

She swallowed, and the lukewarm water was as divine as the first spring rain. She wanted more, though her battle trained mind told her to sip.

Her throat, now damp and soothed, scraped as she searched for her voice.

"Where am I?" Her mind was thick with fog. She had

no memory, but her body bespoke a fierce battle. The cup pressed back to her lips, and the life bringing water eased the cacophony in her head.

Finally, her eyes obeyed, and she blinked up at the gentle face of an elderly man. There was something about his eyes and the curve of his smile that reminded Azalea of Deidre. She had never met her husband's grandfather, but this was most definitely Lord Silas. Yet, there was another name, one that belonged rightfully to her now as well.

"Grandad?" Her throat burned, and the name fit the man's tender touch as it trickled out.

"Yes." Silas' smile crinkled his eyes. "How are you feeling? Are you hurting? Too hot?" He fussed with the blankets with one hand and brushed her hair from her face with the other.

"Freezing." Azalea shivered. Her hip twinged and ripped unexpectedly at the tremor. "Pain." She gritted her teeth, whining as she tried to sit up.

"That is to be expected." Silas stood and eased a pillow behind her back. "You lost more blood than I have seen anyone survive. You gave us all quite a scare." He made his way over to a crackling fire and scooped thin liquid from a pot there into a bowl.

The memories flooded back like a rogue wave upon the rocks.

The battle, the Kardens, Nilos in all his godlike fury, and Harvan bleeding out from her dagger in his chest. He had stabbed her. That was the pain in her side. His life stealing magic was why her connection to the wolf was weak.

"Where is Nilos?" she gasped, "Have we defended the city? What of Deidre and Jarrett? Did my father survive?" Her empty lungs sent her head spinning, and Azalea collapsed back into the pillows, whimpering at the burning in her side.

"Ease your worry, child." Silas gave her a gentle smile and settled back into his chair. He stirred the liquid in the bowl. "Now that you are awake, I must get more medicine and food into you. Small sips." The spoon came to her lips, and the thin broth was very nearly the most exquisite thing she had tasted. It warmed its way down her throat, pooling deep in the frigid abyss of her belly. The aftertaste was bitter, as if treated with medicinal herbs. "Nilos is safe, fast asleep in the room next door. Deidre and Jarrett are just down the hall. Your father is with the generals outside of the city."

Azalea scanned the room as she sipped another mouthful of broth, until she found a wooden door. Why was Nilos not in here with her? The sky beyond the curtained windows was dark.

As if he read her mind, Silas smiled.

"You have slept for nearly two days," the old man explained, lifting the spoon to her lips again. "For a day and night my grandson refused to leave your side, but King Brexten finally warned him if you awoke and found he had not rested, you would likely bite him."

"Papa knows me," she sighed. Her grandfather by law dabbed the corner of her lips with a kerchief. "Thank you, Grandad."

"Of course, little blossom," said Silas. "A few more sips, and I shall get you something for the pain."

"What happened?" She swallowed the next spoonful before reaching up to scratch an itch that pestered her cheek. A thin, raised line throbbed under her touch, and the familiar poke of sutures scratched her thumb.

"King Brexten did not permit the healers to fully close the outer layers of your flesh," said Silas. "He said scars are beauty marks, and you would not want to hide the evidence of your victory."

"Papa," grumbled Azalea, but her father was correct.

"What happened up there between you and Harvan?" Silas took a wet rag from a nearby table and dabbed her temple. "You nearly sliced his heart in half." Azalea did not know how she was sweating when she was so cold.

"I almost failed." Azalea winced at the memory of her near defeat, but each painful breath reminded her that she had come out victorious. "If that sound had not startled him, he would have slit my throat." She shifted under the blanket, trying to stretch her aching muscles. "What was that sound? It was more than Nilos' most powerful strike."

"That would be my grandchildren giving Vadros a taste of his own medicine." Silas brimmed with pride.

"Deidre was supposed to stay with Jarrett." Azalea squeezed her eyes shut, trying to recall anything after Harvan's final breath. "Did he not lead them to me?"

"Like I said." Silas chuckled. "My grandchildren. I count your knight amongst them as equally as I count you, little blossom."

He patted her hand, and Azalea squeezed his fingers with what little strength she could muster. Silas pulled a bottle from the floor and poured the contents onto the spoon he fed her with.

"For the pain," he murmured, "It will put you back to sleep."

Azalea sipped the harsh tonic. It stung her throat and dried her tongue, but, by the time she turned her lips into his soft kerchief, darkness dragged her back into its prison.

When Nilos woke, the gray gloaming of dawn had begun creeping into the window. Panic disoriented him for a moment until he realized he was in the Headmaster's rooms of the Arcadius Academy. He scrambled out of his grandfather's bed and crossed to the door of what had once been Deidre's room.

Silas was seated beside Azalea, where he had been for nearly three days. His wrinkled face was lax in sleep, cheek resting where his weathered hand clasped Azalea's on the blanket. Nilos had only seen him so devoted to caring for the sick once before.

When Deidre was twelve, a pox had spread through the students. Deidre had the worst of it, and their grandfather had tended to her day and night. He had not slept until his granddaughter's fever had finally broken, and she had woken up long enough to eat.

Azalea's body was no longer limp with the reaper's grip. Her cheeks were flushed, and her head turned on the pillow. Nilos' heart finally unclenched. He crossed to his sleeping grandfather and touched his shoulder lightly.

"Grandad," he whispered, shaking him gently.

"Nilos." Silas lifted his head and blinked blearily at him. "What is the matter?"

"You go to bed." Nilos smiled at his drowsy nod. "I will attend my wife's sick bed."

Silas patted his hand before standing.

"She is a strong woman," murmured Silas, "She reminds me of your grandmother." He clapped Nilos' shoulder as he made his way from the room.

Nilos took his place in the chair and lifted Azalea's warm hand to his lips. Her head shifted on the pillows, and those beautiful pools of honey met his gaze in a series of slow, strained blinks.

"Good morning, my love," Nilos whispered, kissing her

fingers again.

"Good morning," croaked Azalea, and her raspy voice sang relief to Nilos' soul. "I did not mean to worry you so."

Nilos released her hand to pour water into the empty cup near the bed. He cradled her hair and pressed it to her lips. He had let her get separated from him, and she was apologizing? He would not stand for any guilt from his precious wife.

"I should never have let you out of my sight." He pulled the cup away, chuckling at the scowl she barely managed to. "But, if we both agree to never play a gamble with the reaper again, we can forgive each other."

"What have I missed while I slept?" Azalea lifted, but a whimper escaped her lips. Nilos eased her back down onto the pillows.

"Very little, my love." Nilos longed to crawl up in the narrow bed with his beloved, but she was still recovering. The healers had tended to what they could, but the wound was still sutured until they were certain they had mended all of the internal injuries. "Your father and the High General pushed back whatever remained of the Karden forces to the mountains. General Beakpoint and your mother are keeping them contained there. Without a leader, they have not tried more than sporadic, weak attacks."

"My mother?" Azalea shot up and then keened as she clutched her side. Nilos tried to ease her back down, but his wife growled and snapped her teeth at his arm.

"She left Sanctuary Island as soon as she received word that Harvan and Vadros were defeated." Nilos rubbed her back. She squeezed her eyes shut. "Alastrex is still safe there in the care of the priestesses."

"How are Jarrett and Deidre?" hissed Azalea through

clenched teeth.

"Fine, last I saw them." He stroked her uninjured cheek, coaxing her beautiful eyes open. "Jarrett was loathe to leave your side, but I ordered him to rest or join the efforts to rebuild the city until I sent for him." Azalea turned her cheek into his hand, and, finally, a single tear seeped from her eye. "I thought I would lose you, Azalea. We saved our lands, but I nearly lost you forever." He choked out a sob, leaning in to kiss her softly.

"It will take much more than a madman with a dagger and warped magic to rip me from this world," whispered Azalea. She nipped his lip, and Nilos knew she was whole despite her injuries. "You will never be rid of me, in this lifetime or the next." She swayed for a moment, and Nilos pulled away. Her cheeks flushed, and she hid behind her hair. "My love, I need—" Her eyes drifted around the room. "I need to relieve myself."

"I can carry you." He pulled back the blanket.

Azalea swung her legs over the bed, before he could stop her, and she cried out as her knees buckled. Nilos caught her by the waist and shook his head.

"I said I would carry you."

"Need to walk," huffed Azalea. "Lend me your shoulder. I must stretch my muscles for them to heal."

Nilos nearly protested, but her firm stare silenced it.

"Very well." Nilos braced her as he led her to the washroom. Once he was sure she could manage, he stepped outside the door and waited. When she was finished he tried to help her back to bed.

"No." Azalea grumbled and turned towards the small sofa near the fire. "Tired of laying down, and I am hungry."

Nilos shook his head and helped her to the sofa.

"I will fetch your breakfast." He eased her onto the cushion and retrieved her blanket. "But you must promise to stay right here and not try to walk until I return."

"I am wounded, my love, not incompetent." Azalea slapped at his arm, but he kissed her hair regardless.

When she was safely tucked into the corner cushion, he draped the blanket tenderly around her. After a soft parting kiss, he tore himself away from his wife and slipped quietly into the hall.

Students milled about in their recreational robes, rubbing sleepy eyes or dusty faces as they returned from the city repairs. A few of the younger teens noted him, bowing and mumbling exhausted greetings. He tapped their shoulders in reply, keeping himself from turning back to check on Azalea.

Though it had been nearly nine years since he had wandered the halls, Nilos knew the way to the kitchens by muscle memory.

"Your Majesty!" One of the cooks yelped when he stepped into the room. "Please, go through to the dining hall. We will bring you a meal immediately."

"If you do not mind, I would rather help you prepare something for the Empress." He edged towards the stoves, eyeing the various pots and pans. "Something light but warm. Perhaps oats with honey."

"We are currently cooking some now, Your—"

"Just Nilos please," he insisted, waving a hand. "I am no Emperor in this moment, merely a husband who wishes to tend to his injured wife."

"Then let the cooks do their job, and you put food in your own belly," the cook replied and handed him some bread stuffed with bacon. "Sit there and eat this." He pointed to a table nearby, and Nilos sank into the chair. Another cook had a cup of juice and a bowl of fruit in front of him in moments.

Nilos hurried through his meal, though he preferred to eat with Azalea. He did not want to be rude to the cooks who were already weary with the strain of the Academy serving as the headquarters for those whose homes had been damaged as well as the royal guard.

He was nearing anxious when a cook finally announced his tray was ready. Nilos declined their offers to carry it up.

"The Empress does not want to be fussed over," he explained, "Convincing her to let me fetch her breakfast nearly got me smacked." Finally, the cooks laughed and shooed him from the room.

Nilos found Azalea right where he left her, much to his surprise. Not to his surprise, however, was the fact that she was half asleep with the blanket bundled under her cheek on the arm of the sofa.

"My love." Nilos placed the tray on the low table. She hummed, her eyes drifting open. "I bring sustenance."

Azalea winced as she lifted her head from her blanket. Her side was burning again, but she did not want the tonic to put her back to sleep.

"Does Grandad have anything to treat the pain that will not keep me drowsy?"

"I believe so." Her husband kissed her brow as he handed her a bowl. "Eat your oats, and I will check through his healing supplies."

Azalea pushed through the ache as she lifted the spoon and chanced a small bite. Her injured cheek ached, but she was able to chew the creamy, honeyed oats. It did not take long for him to return.

"Spoon?" asked Nilos, and Azalea surrendered it. He filled

it with a pink liquid, and Azalea hummed at the berry sweet flavor as she sucked it down. "You may feel slightly euphoric in a few minutes, but that will only last about an hour."

Azalea was too famished to speak, when Nilos settled gently on the cushion beside her. He held a cup full of sunfruit juice. She eagerly sipped it between bites, the taste of her home warming a part of her that the oats could not touch. When she finally finished most of her meal, the weak shakiness in her limbs had stopped, as had the headache and burning pain in her ribs.

A giddy excitement bubbled up inside of her, allowing her to rest her head against his shoulder.

"I want to go out into the city." Azalea tugged her husband's shirt. "I want to see my father."

"Are you sure?" Nilos' face was incredulous as he kissed her brow for what felt like the hundredth time since she woke. "It is the medicine. You should rest more until the healers come in to check if your wound can be fully sealed?"

"A leader should be amongst the people," insisted Azalea. Nilos shook his head, but she tugged his shirt again. "I could see one of the healers tending to the wounded there."

"Very well." Nilos tapped her nose softly. "You will not walk all that way, so do not even ask."

Azalea knew, even in her floating contentment, that there was no point in trying to refute that argument. With how numb her right hip had grown, there was no way she would make it further than the first block. Instead, she grabbed him by the front of his shirt and pulled him in for a kiss.

Nilos smiled. Azalea's lips were soft, warm, and alive against his own. He longed to take her into his arms, but he would not risk aggravating her wounds. Instead he stroked her hair and savored the kiss for a few moments, then broke free with a smile.

"Like I said, you are not walking."

He helped Azalea into a warm, loose tunic, taking care not to jostle the bandages wrapped around her sutures. Then, into a fleece lined pair of soft and flexible riding pants and boots she went. Finally, he scooped his arm around her waist and guided her into the hall.

"Azi!" Jarrett's voice rang down the hall, and Nilos laughed as the knight rushed towards them. "Of course you are already on your feet, though you nearly died."

"I am forcing him to take me to visit Papa," giggled Azalea as the knight took her into his arms with a gentle touch. Nilos did not protest the embrace or the kisses that Jarrett rained onto her hair. "Care to join us?"

"I will fetch us horses." Nilos smiled. "Bring her down to the main doors, and do not let her walk unassisted." He fixed his Empress with a look. "Even if she bites you."

Hurrying ahead, he signaled two of the students returning from the city for their horses, and soon he was on the stallion accepting Azalea from her knight. She could not hide the pain from him as she gave a forced smile but asking her to return to bed was a worthless endeavor.

Azalea took in the destruction and hope around them. Evidence of the battle was there in burned building and destroyed homes, but they were not what took her breath away. It was the people.

Zelarian citizens and Tyldonian soldiers alike were laboring side by side in the light snow to repair the wounded city.

"We sent mages down to Tyldon as well," murmured Nilos against her ear, "Some of the villages near the border need to be rebuilt from the ground up, but militias of civilians kept the Karden from advancing too far into your homeland."

Riding hurt, but not as bad as walking. So, it was easy for Azalea to fight it back and observe as they made their way to the gate. The smell of smoke grew more pungent, and billows of black came from various points outside the walls. When they made it past the partially constructed gates, she found the cause.

Piles of dead Kardens were being burned. Amongst a group of soldiers stacking firewood was a familiar pair of golden braids down a scarlet cape. The High General saw them and clapped her father on the back.

Nilos knew what was going to happen before he could stop her. So, when Azalea kicked their horse into a canter, he laughed and held her tightly on the stallion's bare back. He and his father-in-law had reached a mutual level of respect over the past couple of days, but there was no denying the relief and adoration in the man's eyes as Azalea leaned forward and fell into his embrace.

"I knew you would be up and around." King Brexten buried his face in his daughter's hair, and it was the first time Nilos had seen the man genuinely smile in person. "We could not keep you in bed even as a child."

"I missed you, Papa." Azalea clung to her father, savoring the strength of his arms and the way his scruffy jaw tickled her hair. Despite her numbly throbbing side, she was suddenly ten in pigtails and ribbons. "I could not stay in bed without checking on my people."

"I think you will find our warriors are recovering well." Her father stroked her hair and gestured out at the soldiers around them.

Azalea cast her gaze out to the tents sprawled along the hills, some scarlet and gold, others silver and blue. They mingled together, and soldiers and mages came and went from both.

"No, Papa." She reached back for Nilos' hand. "All of my people." Her husband squeezed her fingers and lifted it to his lips.

Azalea took in the two men holding her hands. One worshiped her with adoration and love. The other beamed at her with a mixture of pride and incredulity.

"You really do love him?" Her father raised an eyebrow at her.

"Yes, Papa." Azalea ignored her pain, and she pulled Nilos closer so she could loop her arms through both of theirs. "I love Nilos with everything I have."

"Well then." Her father reached past her to take Nilos' hand. "I think It is about time our two countries came to a permanent alliance, and not just one for war."

Nilos grasped Brexten's forearm in Tyldonian tradition.

"I wholeheartedly agree." He nodded down to the woman grinning up at both of them, her eyes glassy from the tonic he had given her. "But first, our wolf needs to see the healers."

The Dawn of Hope

It took nearly two weeks after the attack on the city before the scholars researching the Rift spell finally formulated a new one. The only issue they had to work around was preventing a Zelarian mage and a Tyldonian warrior from going into the Rift and sacrificing themselves. Nilos was certain there must be another way. So, when they brought the new solution before them, the four rulers could not have been more pleased.

They rode out with King Brexten to join Queen Violet and her army at the Heirlight mountains, where they had forced the half legion of surviving Karden back over their bridges of corpses and mud into the wasteland on the other side of the vast canyon.

Azalea was impressed by the effort that the scholars from both countries had put into developing a new spell. It would not only keep their lands safe from any other dangers that might dwell in the toxic waste of Vanar, but it insured a lasting alliance between both nations. It was simple, in essence, but it required a massive amount of magic from Zelarum and blood from the soldiers of Tyldon.

They and her parents agreed that it was the best solution that could be drawn up, given the alternative. Every year, one hundred and twenty Tyldonian soldiers would go to the temple of the Sun and donate a single pint of blood. That blood would be used to forge exactly one hundred and twenty arrows. The soldiers would then ride to the Heirlight Mountains, where they would meet one hundred and twenty mages. The mages would release their magic onto the arrows as they were fired. Then the arrows would act as magical nails holding the Rift closed.

The only way to break the spell would be to either not repeat the ritual or to have the exact same two hundred and forty people from that year's ritual recall the arrows from the air between the lands.

Azalea stood with her mother as Nilos joined her father at the edge of the canyon. Next year she would partake in the ritual. Despite having been tended to by the best healers of both lands, the four-day journey from Arcadius had left her tired and sore. She and her wolf could also not stop worrying that they were missing something important, though they could not figure out what it was. So, she watched in anticipation to see her mother's reaction to Nilos summoning his magic to him.

When the lightning began sparking off his skin and hair, her mother let out an impressed chuff.

"He is stunning," whispered Violet, when Nilos' lightning fused with Brexten's arrow. "Stormwielder indeed."

The air above the ravine that separated their countries from Vanar shimmered in a kaleidoscope of colors. Everywhere the arrows landed in the barrier, a beam of light shot out over their heads. Once the skies cleared, there was nothing to show that the Rift even existed except for one hundred and twenty tiny twinkling lights far overhead.

A mining village nestled at the base of the mountains hosted a victory celebration. The moon hung full over the dale on the fourth and final evening of the feast.

As Azalea was dressing for dinner in their sprawling tent, she stopped as she, again, felt as if something was missing, something that should be important. The Wolf in her mind gave no hint of a threat or danger. So, she said nothing to Nilos and joined him at dinner.

Nilos had never felt so lighthearted and happy. Though he missed his mother terribly, his wife's joy at being with her family and the thrill of victory kept his grief at bay. When he returned home, he would give himself space to mourn her fully. Yet, as the celebrations stretched into their fourth night, he found his cheerful Empress had once again grown quiet and drowsy despite the music and frivolity.

His concern only sharpened when he noted her meal had hardly been touched. When Azalea excused herself from the table, looking pale around her lips, he followed after her to the edge of the village into the woods.

Azalea braced one hand against a tree, vomiting through quiet sobs.

"Sweet goddess?" whispered Nilos, pulling her braid from her shoulder and rubbing her back. "Are you all right love?" Azalea was never one to be ill, even when faced with the worst of death.

"How long has it been since we left Sardit?" she whimpered before another round of heaving racked through her. Nilos held her gently, pulling her skirts free from the sick pooling on the leaves.

"A month," he replied, "Maybe a few days more? Why?"

Azalea staggered upright, her face red and watery from the tears staining her cheeks.

"I know what's missing," she gasped, swaying in place and clinging to his arms.

"What are you talking about?" he asked, pulling a kerchief from his shirt and dabbing her lips. Azalea's eyes filled with tears, glittering golden diamonds in the full moon above.

"I noticed, in Arcadius and again tonight, that something was missing." She croaked out another sob, as a watery smile formed under his gentle touches. "It did not feel dangerous. I thought, perhaps, it was forgetting to order the troops to do something or even to sign a missive, but I was wrong."

"What was missing?" Nilos shoved his kerchief back into his pockets and cupped her cheeks as Azalea laughed.

"My courses, Nilos." She wrapped her arms around him, and Nilos' stomach sank then soared. "My courses were due last week, but they did not come."

"Azalea?" He could not tear his gaze away from the golden glow in her eyes. "Are you saying you are with child?"

"I believe I may be." She lowered her hand to her belly, stroking it between them. "Last night, remember, I was so sensitive when we made love, and my breasts were too tender to be handled."

"A baby?" Nilos wanted to howl, but he could barely find his voice when he lifted Azalea by her waist and spun her beneath the sparkling stars. Dread stole his joy in an instant, and he froze in their ecstatic twirl. "You were injured. Azalea, you lost so much blood. I want you to see a midwife, immediately."

"Is there one in the village?" Azalea's joy edged with terror as her wolf whined and circled a new glow deep within her core. What if what was missing was the baby's growth? "Send for her and my parents. Please."

"Come with me." Nilos took her hand and guided her

towards the lights of the festival.

Her mother caught her eye immediately, her expression keen and curious. Azalea gestured towards her father and then towards the tents. Violet nodded and touched her husband's arm.

Nilos stopped a young girl of about six who was chasing a puppy nearby.

"Fetch the village midwife to our tent." The girl stumbled to a stop, her green eyes wide. Azalea pulled a handful of coins from her purse and pressed them into the girls' palm. "And tell no one why." Until she was sure, she did not want to get the hopes of the people raised.

They made their way to the tent just as her parents reached them.

"What's wrong?" asked her father as he fell into step on her right.

"Nothing," laughed her mother. "I know that expression well."

Azalea's cheeks burned when her mother pushed her and Nilos into the warm, lamp lit interior of the tent.

A few moments later, there was a knock on the outer pole.

"Come in!" she and Nilos called together.

A woman who appeared to be in her mid-sixties lifted the flap and stepped inside. She curtsied low and smiled at them. "You requested me, your Majesties?"

"Yes, Mrs?" Nilos let the question hang in the air.

"Hannah." The midwife smiled. "How may I be of assistance?" Her clever, sapphire eyes were dancing between him and Azalea in a knowing way.

"We would like to know if you would be able to check and see if Empress Azalea is with child," Nilos explained. Behind him, Brexten gave a strangled yelp.

"But of course." Hannah grinned broadly and waved Azalea to a cushion in the corner of the tent. "Please, Your Majesty, remove your cloak." Then she looked back over her shoulder. "King Brexten, if you would avert your eyes, I need to ask her to also remove her bodice."

Azalea settled onto the cushion and unwrapped the folds of her warm dress. Her heart pounded out a tattoo when the midwife parted her supportive undergarments to expose her stomach. She clung to Nilos' hand as he stood beside her.

The midwife's touch was gentle and warm as she knelt and pressed her palms against Azalea's pelvis. A soft yellow light glowed under her skin, filling Azalea's senses with the scent of warm grain and soft, herbal balms. Deep in her abdomen, something tickled in response, and the wolf in her soul jumped and yipped in joy around the tickle.

Nilos held his breath, and Violet smacked his arm. He let it out with a grunt. Azalea's face was radiant, as the mid-wife's glow spread under her skin to glisten from her lips. Then it shimmered away after Hannah pulled her palms back and stood. He tore his gaze from Azalea to meet her eyes, and the woman looked down at Azalea. He mimicked her, his heart beating its way into his throat. Azalea's face split into a broad grin at the unspoken conversation.

Finally, Hannah smiled, and Nilos's storm whipped into a joyous gale as the old woman let out a laugh. His wife tugged her undergarments closed and swiftly re-wrapped her bodice.

"Indeed, Your Majesty, I am confident in reporting that Empress Azalea is with child." She inclined her head, and Nilos bent to haul his giggling wife up for a heated kiss.

"She is in the very early stages," continued Hannah while

King Brexten and Queen Violent laughed and hugged each other behind her. "I almost did not feel the babe, but it is there." She curtsied once again to them both. "It is healthy and growing well." Then she tapped her lips. "I shall say nothing until the official announcement, of course. Congratulations to you both on this joyous event."

Nilos barely heard her over the giggles from mother and daughter and the booming laugh of his father-in-law.

He was going to be a father.

The gods had heard his mother's prayers, and he knew that she and his father would be proud had they been here. It was more than he could ever have dreamed of. So, he willingly went into Violet's embrace and accepted her warm, motherly kisses across his cheeks.

Azalea twirled under her father's arm while he danced her around the tent. She was beyond overjoyed. She and Nilos would have a child, despite all they had endured and the horrors they had faced. Both of her kingdoms were at peace and would be until the end of time. How the gods had thought to bless her so greatly, she did not know.

She squealed when her father scooped them all into a hug, and she wiped the tears of pride that rolled across his scarred cheeks.

Their lands flourished, as did Azalea's pregnancy. The borders between the kingdoms were opened, and the tariffs and trade taxes were driven to near nothing.

When Azalea reached her fourth month in pregnancy, both nations met in the new trade city, Dawnfrost, that was being erected with the border running through the center.

A week-long celebration was held then, and it was there that the four leaders signed an eternal alliance between their people. It was the first city where both citizens of Zelarum and Tyldon lived together in harmony after nearly seven centuries of distrust, and it was on its dedication day that she announced her pregnancy to both lands. It was also there, in Dawnfrost, on Princess Idris' first birthday that she was presented to both nations publicly for the first time since her howl-filled and thunder-guarded birth.

In the midst of her birthday feast, Prince Alastrex plucked her from her chair, sat her on the royal table, and stuck a tiny, wooden bow in her hands. Before Azalea or Nilos could take it from Idris, her six-year-old uncle helped her draw back the narrow string.

The minuscule arrow flew over the table in a burst of golden light. It stuck in a purple berry on King Brexten's plate and exploded in a cloud of glittering, heated solar magic that scalded the face of her stunned grandfather.

The tiny hall grew quiet for a moment, but the crowd erupted into a cheer. Little Idris clapped her hands and howled her amusement to her grinning parents.

About the Author

Tabitha is a queer, neurodivergent author from Florida. She is the mother of one human child and one fur-baby. She achieved her MFA in English and Writing with a concentration in fiction from Southern New Hampshire University in May of 2022. She has been teaching English Composition, American Literature, and Creative Writing since February of 2023.

You can connect with me on:

🌐 https://tabithastricklandauthor.com